Burning Love

by

Jana Richards

Burning Love

Cover Art by *Nicola Martinez*

The Wild Rose Press
PO Box 708
Adams Basin, NY 14410-0706
Visit us at www.thewildrosepress.com

Publishing History
First Faery Rose Edition, 2010
Print ISBN 978-1-5092-0452-6
Digital ISBN 978-1-62830-406-0

Published in the United States of America

Riley looked into her beautiful blue eyes and her smiling face and did the only thing he was capable of doing at the moment.

He kissed her.

Maybe later, he told himself, when sanity returned, he'd think of a hundred reasons why pulling Iris into his arms, holding her snug against his body, and plundering her soft, sweet mouth was not a good idea. But for now, right now, as she wound her arms around his neck and made tiny sounds of excitement deep in her throat, it felt exactly right.

Heaven. Having Iris in his corner made him believe everything was possible.

He stepped backward toward the stairs, pulling Iris with him, intent on taking her upstairs to his room. He suddenly tripped, nearly losing his balance. He glanced behind him and saw the object he'd stumbled over. A set of luggage sat next to the stairs, still bearing tags from the retailer.

"What the hell is this?"

Iris kissed his neck. "I'm sorry. I should have taken them up to my room."

Iris had bought new luggage for her trip. Her plans hadn't changed.

She's leaving me.

The thought acted as effectively as a bucket of cold water tossed over his head. What was he doing? She was leaving in three weeks and didn't plan to return. The calendar in the kitchen reminded him of that every day. Why start something that would only lead to heartache?

He'd already lost too many people in his life.

And Riley instinctively knew that if he let himself get close to Iris, let himself love her, a part of him would not survive when she left.

Dedication

To my critique partner Janet, for her boundless imagination and unswerving belief in my writing.

Chapter One

Riley Benson's fire truck screeched to a stop in front of an old brick apartment building as smoke belched from a third story window. All was chaos on the normally quiet street in Portland's Pearl District. Firefighters poured water onto the roof of the building from the aerial platform of a ladder truck already on site. Police cars and ambulances flanked both sides of the street, their flashing lights illuminating the night. The air reeked of diesel exhaust and acrid smoke. After five years as a firefighter, the familiar smell sent adrenalin rushing through Riley's veins.

He jumped from the truck when it came to a stop and began unrolling hose. Police attempted to keep onlookers a safe distance away. Residents of the apartment building milled around in various states of undress. Riley caught snippets of angry rumblings from the crowd.

"I'll bet it's that girl from the third floor again. She did this!"

"That woman is dangerous!"

Before Riley could wonder what they were talking about, a woman's shrill scream sounded over all the other noise.

"Someone's still in the building! I saw a woman at the window!"

Another person shouted, "Yes, I saw her too! In the stairwell, on the second floor."

"There she is! She's heading up the stairs!"

"She must be crazy! Why would she run back into a burning building?"

Captain Andrews shouted instructions. "Benson, Carruthers, Smith. Find the woman and get her out."

Riley dropped the hose and ran toward the building's entrance, pulling his breathing apparatus over his face as he scrambled over hoses. Though this fire was mostly smoke and largely under control, that didn't mean it wasn't still dangerous. He led the way as the three firefighters formed a single line and made their way up the stairs. The smoke grew thicker the higher they climbed until Riley could barely see in front of his face.

"Frank, Jim!" Riley called on his radio. "You still with me?"

Riley felt a hand on his leg. "Right behind you."

"Bringing up the rear, Riley."

Reassured, Riley pushed on. A moment later he heard coughing and dropped to his knees, feeling along the wall until he found the woman. He slipped an arm beneath her and hoisted her over his shoulder in the fireman's carry.

"I've got her," he said over the radio. "Let's get out of here."

The woman pummeled his back with her small fists. "No, no! I have to go back! Please, let me go!"

A fit of coughing cut off her words. The firefighters rushed down the stairs and out of the building. As Riley carried the woman across the lawn to a waiting ambulance, a bald man with a paunch wearing boxers and an undershirt pointed an accusing finger at them.

"It's her! It's the girl who started the fire the last time!"

"She should be evicted!"

"We're not safe as long as she lives here," someone else shouted.

Riley hurried to the ambulance and set the woman down just inside the open doors. Was it true? Had she caused a previous fire?

Dave, the EMT, tried to administer oxygen to the woman, but she pushed aside the mask and jumped from the ambulance, ready to make her escape.

"Iris, it's me, Dave. You have to let me help you."

"No, no. Please!" She shoved away the mask once more.

"Riley, give me a hand here, will you?"

"Sure. You know her?"

Dave grinned. "We've met before. Iris here is a pretty rotten cook. When she burns a meal she really burns a meal. I've been a guest at her little midnight *soirées* on previous occasions."

So it was true. Was she some kind of firebug, one of those crazy people who got their thrills by deliberately setting fires?

Riley grasped both of her hands in one of his and wrapped one arm around her waist while Dave placed the mask over her mouth and nose. He tried to ignore the feel of her soft, warm body pressed tightly against his. She struggled to free herself, but it was a lost cause. She couldn't have been more than five-three and maybe a hundred and fifteen pounds. Despite her small stature, her curves were generous. Her breasts strained against the thin material of her T-shirt, her nipples pebbling to hard peaks in the cool night air. Riley could imagine one breast fitting perfectly in the palm of his hand...

Whoa! Where the hell had that come from?

He abruptly loosened his hold and Iris took the opportunity to wrench one arm free and push away the mask. "My cat. I have to find her. She's all I have. Please!"

Finally Riley understood. He looked into her face. Her bright blue eyes stood out starkly against her smoke-blackened face, pleading with him to understand. Tears forged little rivulets of mud down her cheeks. In her eyes he read panic and genuine fear. Anyone who loved her cat as much as Iris obviously did would never deliberately start a fire that might endanger her beloved pet. He had a dog and understood completely. No way had Iris started this fire on purpose.

"What's your cat's name?"

"Whiskers," she rasped before a fit of coughing stopped her.

"I'll find her."

At his nod, Dave placed the mask over her mouth and nose again. This time Iris didn't fight him. She sat quietly and closed her eyes as if all the fight had drained from her body.

Riley turned and headed back to the apartment building. He spoke to his captain.

"Cap, I'm going back in. The girl says her cat is still in there."

"Pets often go into hiding during a fire," Captain Andrews said. He shook his head. "This is the third fire we've responded to at Iris Jennings' apartment this year. It's a miracle no one has been seriously injured."

Riley glanced back at Iris and nodded glumly. He couldn't let a pair of pretty blue eyes distract him from doing his job, and right now that job was to find her cat.

As he checked his air pack on the front step of the building, he heard a faint mewing. Riley removed his helmet and listened, straining to hear the cat over the noise of the emergency vehicles. After a moment he heard the mewing again and followed the sounds around the side of the building into some shrubs.

"Whiskers? Is that you? C'mere, Whiskers."

A small gray cat with a white face and paws stepped tentatively from behind her hiding place in the bushes. Riley reached a gloved hand toward her, and she rubbed her face against it and purred, as if grateful for rescue. Riley scooped her up and carried her back to the ambulance, hoping the cat belonged to Iris. He didn't want to examine too closely his need to ease her distress.

Iris sat just inside the ambulance, her head bowed and her shoulders slumped in utter despair. The oxygen mask was gone. She looked small and helpless as she clutched the thin blue blanket wrapped around her shoulders. Riley fought the urge to wrap her in his arms and keep her safe. He cleared his suddenly dry throat, shaken by his thoughts.

"Is this Whiskers?"

Iris lifted her head, her gaze colliding with his. When she saw the cat in his arms her despair dissipated, forgotten along with the blanket as she jumped from the ambulance.

"Oh, Whiskers!" She reached for the cat and cuddled it in her arms. "I thought I'd lost you."

Fresh tears poured from her eyes, making her cheeks even muddier. "Is she okay?"

"She's fine. I think she got out of the apartment faster than you did. I found her outside."

Iris laughed and hugged the cat close. "It's a good thing you're smarter than me."

Riley watched Iris whisper reassurances to Whiskers, her clear blue eyes sparkling with tears. Aside from her amazing eyes, there was nothing remarkable about her. Black soot covered her from head to toe, and she smelled strongly of smoke. So why did he feel this pull toward her?

Get a grip, Benson.

He turned to Dave. "Does Iris need to go to the hospital?"

"I'd like to have her checked more closely at the hospital, maybe have her stay overnight for observation."

"No, I'm fine, really," Iris protested. "No permanent damage. I don't need to go to the hospital."

"You inhaled a lot of smoke, Iris," Riley said.

"You should listen to Dave."

"I'm fine. See? I'm not even coughing anymore."

"Smoke inhalation can be tricky—"

"No! I'm not going to the hospital."

Dave glanced at Riley and sighed. "All right, but I strongly advise you to visit your doctor as soon as possible."

Iris nodded, rubbing her cheek against Whiskers' fur. Riley suspected the reason she didn't want to go to the hospital was because of the cat. Now that Iris's apartment was uninhabitable, Whiskers was as homeless as she was. What would she do with the cat if she were stuck in the hospital?

A Cadillac squealed to a halt next to the ambulance, and a short bald man hopped out. Riley recognized him immediately and his jaw clenched in anger. Joe Gardiner, landlord, real estate developer, and first class money-grubbing louse. Riley knew from bitter experience what Gardiner was capable of.

"What the hell is going on here?" Gardiner bellowed. A second later he spied Iris. "You! I should have known you'd be responsible for this!"

He made his way toward her, vengeance in his eyes. Riley stepped in front of him, blocking his access to Iris.

"Are you trying to ruin me? We just finished the repairs from the last fire."

Iris held her cat close. "It was an accident. I'm sorry."

"Once is an accident. Three times is arson!" Gardiner tried to go around Riley but he stepped in front of him once more.

"I want you out! Now! You'll never rent one of my properties again, and I'll make damn sure no one else rents to you either."

"I'm so sorry," Iris said. "I don't know what happened. I turned on my stove to make a grilled cheese sandwich, and the next thing I knew my apartment was full of smoke. It was an accident, I swear."

"You'll never have another accident in one of my buildings. Consider yourself evicted, effective immediately."

"My things—"

"You'll find what's left of them out on the front lawn tomorrow."

Iris lifted her chin a fraction. Gathering her cat close, she walked away from the apartment building to a chorus of boos and hisses from her angry neighbors. Riley ran after her.

"Iris, wait. Do you have someplace to stay? The department can help you if you need it."

She didn't look at him. "I'll be fine. My friend lives just around the corner. Whiskers and I can stay with her."

"Are you sure? Do you need a ride?"

Iris's chin quivered as she struggled to hold back tears, giving him a glimpse of the vulnerability that lay just under the surface of her bravado. Without thinking, he reached out to touch her. Her skin felt warm and alive under his hand, and his heart gave an involuntary leap. She glanced at his hand on her arm and then lifted her gaze to meet his, a determined smile on her lips.

"You're very kind, but I'm fine. Thank you."

Riley dropped his hand and watched her disappear into the night with her back straight and her head held high.

His chest tightened at the sight of Iris walking alone down the street. Did she really have a friend around the corner willing to take her in? Would she be okay?

Enough! Iris Jennings was not his responsibility.

Her carelessness likely caused this fire and probably two others. He was damn lucky he didn't live anywhere near her.

****

Meanwhile, in a far, far away place...

"Angelica, now what have you done? I told you not to open the Earth window!"

Angelica watched with Hildegard as firefighters hosed downed a smoke-blackened apartment suite on other side of the window. She frowned. This hadn't gone quite as well as she'd hoped.

"What in the name of St. Peter were you doing? I only left you alone for ten minutes!"

"I was matching a couple of soul mates," Angelica said, forcing cheerfulness into her voice. "After all, that's what we do here in Relationship Division, isn't it?"

"Wrong," Hildegard said, crossing her arms. "It's what *I* do here in Relationship Division. *You're* supposed to be dusting my office, not creating havoc on Earth."

Angelica stamped one small foot, all pretense of cheerfulness gone. "I've been here in Heaven for ages. I'm supposed to be an angel-in-training, but nobody will train me to do anything important!"

"With good reason! You could have killed somebody with that fire."

"I had the fire under complete control the whole time," Angelica said. As soon as the lie slipped from her mouth, her truth bracelet lit up like a firecracker, its shrill siren assaulting her ears. Stupid truth bracelet. Every angel-in-training wore one, but hers got more of a workout than most.

"Okay, so maybe the fire was a little bit out of control," she admitted. The truth bracelet silenced at once. "But I did everything else by the book. Honestly."

Hildegard marched to the filing cabinet and pulled out a folder bulging with papers. Angelica groaned. Not the file again. Was that thing going to follow her around Heaven for the rest of the afterlife?

Hildegard flipped through the papers. "You've been found unsuitable for every job you've been given in Heaven." She pulled a sheaf of papers from the file. "Look at this. When you were assigned to Messenger Division you mixed up a couple of communications. A ninety-year-old great-grandmother was told she was going to have a baby."

"It was an accident. I put the wrong message in the envelope addressed to the great-grandmother." The incident had ended her career in Messenger Division. It had been a bad day for her and she suspected it hadn't been so good for the great-grandmother either.

"Then there was the debacle in the Avenger Division," Hildegard continued.

Angelica closed her eyes in misery. "Do we have to rehash this again? Can't we just let bygones be bygones?"

From the set of Hildegard's jaw, Angelica guessed the answer to that question was no. Hildegard was as by-the-book an angel as she'd met in Heaven. Everything about her screamed businesslike efficiency, from her sensible black loafers and brown tweed suit, to her steel rimmed glasses and severely pulled back hairstyle. Only the elegant lines of her beautiful wings softened her look.

Hildegard scowled. "You nearly sent the entire Avenger squad to exact retribution on a poor old corn farmer in Iowa instead of a drug lord in New York City."

"Okay, so I got the names mixed up. Johnson, Johnston. Anyone could have made that mistake."

"And yet no one but you ever has." Hildegard flipped through the pages. "Ah, my personal favorite. Divine Intervention Division. They're still trying to put their computer system back together. How did you manage to foul up an entire database? You were only there one day."

"I work fast, I guess." Angelica had no idea what happened. She'd accessed the database to do a simple search for one of the senior angels and somehow she'd managed to disable the whole system.

"What are we going to do with you, Angelica? Aside from being totally inept, you're always late for everything."

"It takes time to put this look together." Angelica gave her blonde curls a little shake, making them bounce. "Do you know how long it takes to get my hair just right? And selecting the perfect outfit can't be rushed."

Angelica smoothed the silk of her Versace gown. One of the best perks in Heaven was having access to the fashions of dearly departed designers.

"Some of the division heads are saying you should be placed in Service Division."

"What! No, not Service Division! I can't spend eternity cleaning and cooking for other angels." She held out her newly manicured hands to Hildegard. "Do these look like the hands of an angel destined for a life in service?"

"You are far too vain for your own good." Hildegard shuffled through the file. "Your Heaven entrance exams said you tested off the charts for vanity. But according to St. Peter you do have some redeeming qualities. You scored well for empathy and kindness."

Angelica beamed. "Thank you."

"You also scored extremely high on the stubbornness scale."

"Oh. Is that bad?"

"Sometimes. But sometimes stubbornness means you'll stick with a project to the end."

"Does that mean I can stay here with you in Relationship Division?" Angelica clapped her hands in glee. "It's going to be so much fun working here."

"I didn't say that. Don't start picking out the

curtains for your new office just yet."

Hildegard closed the file and placed it back in the cabinet. She glanced at the Earth window once more.

"Wait a minute. Isn't that Iris Jennings? I was working on her file before I got called away to a meeting. What have you done?"

"I told you," Angelica said, mustering her tattered confidence. "I was matching her with her soul mate."

Hildegard hit the rewind button and watched as the whole scene unfolded, from the start of the fire to Iris's solitary walk in the dark.

"You nearly burned down the building and put everyone in danger. Not to mention Whiskers the cat!" Hildegard shook her head in disbelief. "If anything had happened to Whiskers it would have been unforgivable."

"But everything turned out okay. Everybody, including Whiskers, is fine. I had to resort to drastic measures so Iris could meet her soul mate."

"I've already matched her with her soul mate!" Hildegard said, her voice rising in irritation. She snapped her fingers and an extremely attractive male mortal with dark curly hair and laughing brown eyes grinned at them from the other side of the window. "This is Antonio from Milan. Iris is heading to Greece in six weeks to work on a cruise ship in the Mediterranean. Antonio will be working on the same ship. They're going to fall in love immediately and forever. End of story, happily ever after."

"No, it's not happily ever after," Angelica insisted. "I saw Iris's file sitting on your desk and I peeked inside. Antonio's not right for her." She had felt it the moment she'd looked into Iris's eyes.

"I matched them on a hundred points of compatibility, like I do all my matches. It's all very scientific," Hildegard said defensively. She picked up

Iris's file. "Look. They're perfect for each other. Both of them love travel and adventure. She'd be bored comatose if I matched her with a homebody."

"No, you're wrong," Angelica said. She snapped her fingers and brought Iris back to the window. The girl's anxiety and loneliness reached out to her and grabbed her by the throat. "I can *feel* it. She needs a home and security much more than she needs adventure. Yes, she loves to travel, but she needs someone to come home to. She wants a man who'll always be there for her."

"I've been doing this for a long time and I say Iris and Antonio are simpatico," Hildegard said. "You can't just waltz in here and tell me how to do my job."

"If you're so good at your job," Angelica countered, "how come so many mortals get divorced?"

"It's not my fault." Hildegard straightened to her full height and gave her wings an impatient shake, her face registering her annoyance. "I make excellent matches. If the mortals choose to look elsewhere there is nothing I can do to stop them. If you'd studied the policy manual like I told you, you'd know that we here in Relationship Division are allowed to orchestrate the first meeting between our soul mates but after that it's all up to them. The Divine Leader has forbidden us from any further interference. After all, mortals have free will. Far be it from me to question the Divine Leader's directives."

From the tone of her voice, Angelica suspected Hildegard didn't exactly agree with the Divine Leader. Perhaps she wasn't the by-the-book angel Angelica believed her to be. Maybe she had a touch of rebel in her after all.

"Hildy, matching soul mates is what I'm supposed to be doing here in Heaven, I'm sure of it. This is where I'm supposed to be."

Hildegard folded her arms across her chest, one eyebrow rising skeptically. "Oh, really."

"Yes, really. I can *feel* when two people belong together. Why don't we work together? With your scientific method and my creative genius we can't lose."

Hildegard burst out laughing. "You *are* vain. What am I going to do with you Angelica?"

"You're going to give me a chance to prove myself," Angelica said, seizing her opportunity. She grasped Hildegard's hand and pressed it between both of hers. "Let me prove to you that the match I made for Iris Jennings is the best one for her. If she isn't madly in love by the end of six weeks, I will tender my resignation here in Relationship Division and immediately report for duty in Service Division."

"You're serious." Hildegard sounded surprised.

"Completely."

Hildegard stared into her eyes, her expression unreadable. "So who did you have in mind for Iris?"

She's considering it! Angelica could barely contain her excitement. "He's right there. The second firefighter from the left. Riley Benson."

"Well," Hildegard said dryly. "I'll give you points for irony. Matching a girl who's prone to starting fires with a firefighter. By the way, this fire, was that Iris or did you give her a little help?"

"A little of both. Iris put the pan on the stove to heat. I made her forget about it. I wanted Iris and Riley's first meeting to be unforgettable."

Hildegard snorted. "I'm sure it was. What makes Riley a better match for Iris than Antonio?"

"Riley needs Iris. Antonio doesn't. And Iris needs Riley. She needs security in her life, whether she realizes it or not. They even live in the same city. Is that kismet or what?"

"Okay, suppose I go along with this ridiculous plan. At the moment Riley thinks Iris is a crazy firebug. How are you going to change his mind about her? For that matter, how are they even going to meet again? You've had your one chance for a first meeting."

"I have faith," Angelica said. "These two belong together. Somehow the universe will make it happen."

"As long as *you* don't make it happen, Angelica," Hildegard warned. "Setting up a second meeting is totally against policy."

"I know."

"I'm serious Angelica. I will only consider your crazy plan if you solemnly promise to obey all the rules, including the provision banning second meetings."

Angelica held up her right hand. "I solemnly promise I will not set up a second meeting."

"Good. What about the other rules? Under no circumstances are we allowed to go to Earth to befriend, coach, or otherwise influence our matches. The Divine Leader absolutely forbids it."

"If we can't go to Earth, how do we know if the match is working?"

"No problem." Hildegard snapped her fingers and a picture of an old house in the middle of extensive renovations appeared at the Earth window. "This is Riley's house in Portland, Oregon. We can monitor the situation from here. Do you agree to follow the rules?"

"I agree to follow the rules."

"Good. Then in that case I agree to give you a chance to prove yourself with this match you've made between Iris and Riley. If the match works, you'll stay here and work with me in Relationship Division. But if they are not madly in love and totally committed by the end of six weeks, Iris will go on her Mediterranean cruise and be matched with Antonio, and you will go to Service Division. Do we have a deal?"

Hildegard held out her hand. Angelica took a

deep breath. Her whole future in Heaven depended on Iris and Riley and the accuracy of her intuition. Angelica simply couldn't allow them to languish in loneliness. She needed to fight for them, whatever the risk to her.

But if she was wrong, if they weren't soul mates—

Angelica shivered. She couldn't bear to think of it. She was far too pretty to wear one of those horrid Service uniforms.

She shook Hildegard's hand. "Yes, we have a deal."

Hildegard sighed. "Heaven help us."

Chapter Two

Riley's heart tripped over itself when he answered an insistent knock at his door. Surprise didn't come close to expressing what he felt when he discovered Iris Jennings on his front porch. The woman who'd occupied his thoughts for the past week wore a deer-in-the-headlights expression, obviously as shocked to see him as he was to see her.

Buddy let out a volley of sharp barks, picking up on Riley's tension. Sigmund Freud had nothing on Buddy when it came to recognizing anxiety.

"Buddy, sit."

The black Lab quieted immediately and sat obediently at his feet. Iris gave Riley a wan smile.

"Well, at least you didn't sic the dog on me."

Riley folded his arms across his chest and leaned against the door frame, attempting a nonchalant air. "Iris Jennings. What a surprise. My work doesn't usually follow me home."

"I'm sorry. In all the confusion of the fire I've forgotten your name."

"Riley Benson." It was humbling to know she didn't remember his name. What on earth was Iris Jennings doing at his house? And if she didn't know his name, how had she found him?

"I never got a chance to thank you for saving Whiskers."

For the first time Riley realized Iris carried a plastic cat carrier in one hand.

"Whiskers got herself out. Which is more than I can say for you."

"Right. I never thanked you for that either." She

lifted her gaze and looked into his face. The amazing blue eyes that haunted his dreams stared at him with earnest gratitude. "Thank you for saving my life, too."

Riley swallowed, his throat suddenly dry. "You're welcome."

He'd drown in those eyes if he wasn't careful. For the past week he'd thought about her, worried about her, and had come perilously close to searching for her. Riley liked to be in control. The fact that he had no control where Iris was concerned scared the hell out of him.

He cleared his throat and looked pointedly at his watch. "It's been nice talking to you Iris, but if you'll excuse me I've got a lot of work to do."

He started to shut the door.

"No, wait." Iris stuck her foot in the door, wincing when the heavy wood met her sneaker-clad foot. "I need to talk to you about the room you have for rent."

Finally it made sense. He'd placed an ad in the paper offering a room for rent, hoping to bring in a little extra cash to finish renovations. So far he'd had no takers and he was getting a little desperate.

But not that desperate. The idea of living with Iris, her bedroom just across the hall from his, made Riley break out in a cold sweat.

"You're kidding, right? You want me to rent you a room? You caused three fires at your last place. I'd have to be out of my mind to let you anywhere *near* my house."

"Look, I know I'm not ideal roommate material." She took a step closer, her gaze imploring. "I just need a place to sleep and store my things for the next six weeks and then I'm leaving Portland."

He couldn't think with Iris so close. Hell, he could barely form a coherent sentence. The light floral scent of her perfume tantalized his senses, intoxicating him. Riley drank in the sight of her, from the bright turquoise scarf holding back her dark hair to the colorful skirt in shades of blue and green that swirled around her ankles. She reminded him of beautiful, exotic gypsy.

A gypsy who could steal his heart without a second thought.

"I don't think so. Goodbye, Iris."

He started closing the door again.

"No! Please, listen!"

This time she managed to wedge the plastic cat carrier in the door. Whiskers howled in protest as the door made contact. Buddy's ears stood at attention.

"Iris, I really don't have time for this."

"I don't have any place to go!" Her chin trembled and tears rolled down her cheeks. Riley's heart squeezed painfully at her distress. "Joe Gardiner had me black-listed with every landlord in the city. No one will rent to me. He sued me for the damages. I convinced him to take a cash settlement, but now all my savings are gone and I don't get paid for another week so I can't pay for a hotel room. I'm staying with my friend, but her boyfriend is allergic to Whiskers and wants me out. I'm desperate."

How could he turn her away? At least it was only for six weeks. What could happen in six weeks?

Iris mopped her eyes with a tissue, embarrassed that once again she'd turned into a blubbering idiot in front of this man. What must he think of her? She hadn't meant to spill her whole sad story. The last thing she wanted was his pity.

But on the other hand, if pity got her and Whiskers a place to sleep tonight, she'd be forever grateful.

Riley's jaw clenched, a frown marring his handsome face. Green eyes the exact shade of a jade carving she'd once seen regarded her warily, taking her measure. A lock of dark curly hair fell over his forehead and Iris's fingers itched to smooth it from his face. Would it feel as silky as it looked?

Iris blinked, wondering where on Earth that thought had come from. Funny, she hadn't noticed how attractive he was on the night of the fire. Of course, she had been a tad preoccupied.

But she remembered the kindness with which he'd treated her. Would that kindness extend to renting her the room? At least he wasn't pushing her out the door anymore. She held her breath.

"Typical Gardiner. It's not enough he bleeds you dry. He wants his pound of flesh as well." He patted Buddy's head. "You said you're waiting to get paid. Where do you work?"

"At Fair Winds Travel. I'm a travel agent."

"You'll be able to afford the first month's rent in a week?"

"Yes." *Was he considering it?*

"So you only need the room for six weeks?"

Hope flared in Iris's heart. "Yes. Then I'm leaving to work on a cruise ship. I don't plan on coming back."

Riley scratched Buddy's ears, all the while watching her. His somber expression told her the decision to rent the room to her was difficult for him. She couldn't blame him. After all, Riley had seen first hand what a lousy tenant she'd been in the past.

He patted the dog's head once more. "What do you say, boy? Think we can put up with these two as roommates for six weeks?"

Buddy sniffed at Whiskers' carrier and then sat back down on his haunches and looked up at Riley as if to say, "If we must."

Riley studied Iris. "Okay you've got yourself a deal. I'll rent you the room on one condition."

"What's that?" Iris held her breath once more.

"Under no circumstances are you allowed to cook anything. Ever. Is that clear?"

She let out her breath and smiled, relief making

her almost giddy.

"Perfectly."

****

Angelica danced a jig around the Hildegard's office. "I'm good, yes I'm good, I'm so good."

"Quit congratulating yourself. They haven't exactly declared undying love for each other."

"Don't be such a downer, Hildy. Now that they're under the same roof it's only a matter of time before they realize they're soul mates."

"You didn't have anything to do with getting them under the same roof, did you?" Hildegard cast a suspicious eye toward Angelica.

"I certainly did not." Angelica mustered as much self-righteousness as she was able. "I followed the rules to the letter. I told you the universe would find a way to get them together, Hildy."

"I guess since your bracelet didn't light up, you must be telling the truth. Still, they don't have much time to fall in love. In six weeks she'll be on a cruise ship in the Mediterranean. Then I get a shot at matching her with Antonio." She crossed her arms and frowned. "And don't call me Hildy."

The time crunch was a worry, Angelica had to admit. But she felt so strongly that these two belonged together. Surely, they'd feel it soon too?

Of course they would. And then she'd get herself a cushy job here in Relationship Division. Maybe she'd even be Hildy's boss.

"Not bloody likely," Hildegard said.

"What?"

"There's no way you'll ever be my boss so don't even think about it."

"How did you know I was thinking that?"

Hildegard examined her nails. "A little trick I picked up in Heaven University, along with time shifting and teleporting."

"Wow, that's amazing." Angelica looked at Hildy with a whole new respect. "I want to learn mind

20

reading, too. How do I get into Heaven U?"

"*You* don't. An angel has to be selected to go. Students who have successfully completed their training at Heaven University go on to head divisions and become leaders in Heaven. It's an honor and a privilege to attend."

"I'll get in. You'll see."

Hildegard laughed. "It'll be a cold day in you-know-where before you're selected for Heaven U."

"Humph."

Riley and Iris would soon realize they were soul mates and would be matched for life. And she would be selected for Heaven University and what was more, she'd be their top student.

She stared at Hildegard. *Did you hear that, Hildy?*

Hildegard glared back at her. "Don't call me Hildy."

Chapter Three

"Get that damned cat off of my drapes!"

"It's not her fault! Buddy chased her!"

Only an hour in his house and Riley already regretted his decision to let Iris and Whiskers move in. He'd just hung the stupid drapes in the spare room the previous day and Whiskers had already shredded them to rags.

Riley grabbed Buddy's collar. "From now on keep your cat in your room."

"Fine. Keep your dog *out* of my room." She slammed the door as soon as he'd dragged Buddy into the hallway.

When they got downstairs Buddy circled his bed over and over as if unable to get comfortable. Finally he flopped down with a frustrated "Harrumph." Riley grinned.

"Women, huh? I hear ya, Buddy."

Riley resumed the painstaking procedure of scraping layers of old paint from the beautiful moldings around the doors and windows in the living room. He'd already finished scraping the old paint from the built-in china closet in the dining room, uncovering the fine details of the piece. He only needed to apply some stain and a coating of shellac to return the china closet to its former glory.

Riley stopped and stretched. Only eighty-eight linear feet left to strip. The work was tedious but the results were worth the effort.

The whole house was worth the effort. He'd purchased the house a few months ago, after years of trying. It was located in the Irvington district of

Portland, an area of many fine old craftsman style homes. But his interest extended only to this particular home. This was where his Great Aunt Molly and Great Uncle Claude had given him a home when he'd needed one most.

Maybe that was why he'd let Iris stay, because she was homeless like he'd been. How else did he explain his temporary insanity?

"Can I help?"

Riley turned to see the object of his thoughts standing uncertainly in the doorway. The bright blue of her leggings under an oversized black sweater perfectly matched the blue streak in her dark hair. Iris had a decidedly bohemian style of dressing, but somehow it suited her perfectly.

He sighed. If they were going to co-exist for the next six weeks without killing each other, maybe it would be wise to accept the olive branch Iris tentatively held out to him.

"Sure." He handed her some drywall compound and a trowel. "You can patch these little holes in the wall. I think the previous tenants used the living room as a dart board."

Iris ran her hand over the wall. "I see what you mean. There are hundreds of little holes everywhere. What do I do?"

He opened the container of premixed drywall compound and lifted a dollop onto the trowel before spreading it on the wall. "You just spread it on like this. Try to keep it as thin as possible." He handed the trowel back to Iris.

"How's this?" She applied a small amount of the compound to the wall and smoothed it over some holes, stretching on her tiptoes to reach a spot. Her sweater rose to reveal a perfectly shaped derriere covered by bright blue Lycra.

"Looks good." *And the wall doesn't look bad either*. He cleared his throat and shifted his gaze. *It's only for six weeks*, he told himself. Surely he could survive that long.

"Once all the holes are filled I have to sand, and then prime and paint. It's a slow process," he said.

"This is a huge house for one person. Are you planning to flip it when you're done renovating?"

"No way. I waited a long time to buy this house and I plan to stay here. But it's pretty expensive. That's why I was looking for a roommate."

"Lucky for me you were."

"Whenever other renters came to look at the place and realized they'd be living in a construction zone with no kitchen and only one working bathroom, they left pretty quickly."

"So it was lucky for you I came along."

He grinned at her. "I wouldn't go so far as to say *that*. Like you said, you're not exactly ideal roommate material."

"I guess not." She was silent for a few minutes as she spread the compound in the holes. "I didn't set those fires on purpose, you know. They were stupid accidents. Sometimes I get a little too wrapped up in what I'm reading and I forget I've been cooking. Totally my fault, but I wasn't being malicious."

"I didn't think you were malicious, Iris. Just careless."

"I feel awful about what happened. I know I could have hurt someone. It was just fortunate I didn't."

Riley glanced at her. This was a new side of Iris for him. She was a thoughtful, sincere woman, not the crazy firebug he'd made her into. But he couldn't help teasing her a little.

"I believe you Iris, but I still want you to stay away from my hotplate."

"Don't worry, I've learned my lesson. Your hotplate is safe from me."

Riley laughed. "Good to know."

"Why is this house so important to you?"

"I didn't say it was." Riley rarely talked about his childhood.

"Maybe not in so many words. But you said you waited a long time for this particular house."

She was perceptive, he'd give her that.

"I grew up here. My parents died in a car crash when I was six." He told her how Aunt Molly and Uncle Claude had taken him in. "They weren't young anymore, but they didn't hesitate to adopt me and give me a home. They were as loving a family as I could have asked for."

"They sound like wonderful people."

"They were. There's not a day goes by I don't miss them." Anger engulfed him when he remembered their final years. "I went away to college when I was eighteen. I came home at spring break and discovered Joe Gardiner had convinced them to sell the house to him. I found out later he'd paid them well under market value. He conned two old, trusting people who weren't able to look out for their best interests any longer. The man is scum."

"Ah."

"Ah what?"

She turned to deliver him a level stare. "Ah as in, that's the reason you're letting me stay here. As some kind of payback to Joe Gardiner."

"I don't like the way he operates. Nobody deserves to be homeless. Not even you."

"Thanks. I think."

"Okay, I've spilled my guts," Riley said, eager to change the subject. "Now it's your turn. Have you always lived in Portland?"

"Only since my teens. My parents are artists. We traveled all over the country going to different craft fairs and art shows. Dad sold his paintings and Mom her jewelry. I was twelve before I realized other kids lived in houses instead of VW vans. They're a little eccentric to say the least, but great parents."

"Eccentric, huh? You mean aside from living in a van?"

"Well," Iris said thoughtfully, "I consider myself lucky to be named Iris. My mom told me at one point they considered naming me Venus Fly-Trap."

Riley burst into laughter. "I think you dodged a bullet there."

"Oh, I don't know," Iris said with a grin. "Venus has kind of a nice ring to it, though I'm not so sure about the Fly-Trap part."

"You would have been teased mercilessly in school."

"Luckily I didn't have to worry about school yard bullies because my mom home schooled me. She was actually a pretty good teacher." Iris smiled. "She managed to find a museum or art gallery in whatever town we happened to land in. There was always something interesting to be found."

Fascinating. "How did you end up in Portland?"

"When I was in my early teens my parents decided I needed to go to school on a full-time basis. They settled on Portland because they liked the climate and the arts community here, and we lived in a little apartment downtown until I graduated from high school. We were really happy there." Iris's wistful smile told Riley her parents had given her many happy memories.

"Your parents sound like they were a lot of fun."

"They still are, though I don't get a chance to see them as often as I'd like. At this moment I think they're in California, but it's hard to keep track of them. They must have been nomads in a previous life."

Riley sanded a stubborn bit of old paint from the window molding. "Maybe you were, too. You must have a bit of wanderlust in you to drop your life here and rush off to the Mediterranean."

Iris smiled. "Maybe. But it seemed I was always planning these wonderful vacations for someone else, never for me. I decided it was time to see the world for myself."

They worked in companionable silence for some time until Iris stopped to stretch. Riley looked away, not wanting to stare at her butt again like some hormonal teenager.

"I've done as much of this wall as I can reach," she said. "I'll need a ladder to finish the top."

"You don't have to do that, Iris."

She paused in her stretching to look at him. "I want to. Maybe I want to prove to you that I'm not a total screw-up."

It was on the tip of his tongue to make a flippant remark about it being unlikely he'd ever come to that conclusion. But something in her eyes told him she was serious about changing his opinion of her.

"I'll get the ladder for you."

He brought in the stepladder from the back porch and set it up for her. She climbed up and down the ladder, finishing the patch work in an hour or so. Riley inspected her work.

"Not bad. I think you deserve a break. Would you like a cold drink and a snack?"

"A cold drink would be great, but I thought you didn't have a kitchen. What are we going to eat?"

"I've got a bar-size fridge, a microwave, an electric kettle and a two burner hotplate. I can offer you a reasonably cold soda, microwave popcorn, ramen noodles, or fried eggs. What'll it be?"

Iris laughed and Riley enjoyed the sound of it. For the first time he noticed the lovely shape of her mouth and how her smile lit up her face, animating it with life. When she smiled like that her true beauty shone. He almost wished he could make her laugh again.

"How about a soda and microwave popcorn?"

"Coming right up."

He made the popcorn while she went upstairs to wash the drywall compound off her hands. He brought two cans of soda and the bag of popcorn with him into the living room.

"Dinner is served."

"This is dinner? I thought you said it was a snack."

"These days, this is what passes for dinner around here." He handed her a soda and the popcorn. "Would you like some dinner music?"

"Sure, why not?" She stuck her hand into the bag and pulled out some popcorn.

"I don't have cable or Internet hookup yet so radio is it at the moment." He tuned the radio to his favorite station and smiled when he heard a familiar song.

"How do you feel about George Jones?"

She made a face. "Are you serious?"

For some reason the fact she didn't share his love for country music disappointed him, though why it should matter he couldn't say. Few of his friends liked the same music he did, and the guys at the fire hall teased him mercilessly about it.

Iris sat on the floor with her back against the wall. She offered him the bag of popcorn. "Now if you're talking about George Strait that's a different story. And don't get me started about Keith Urban." She fluttered her eyelashes and fanned her face with her hand. "Be still my heart."

Riley stared at her in surprise, his hand still in the popcorn bag.

Maybe they *could* get through the next six weeks without killing each other.

****

Angelica danced around the office, singing at maximum volume.

"Oh, Riley and Iris are soul mates, they'll be together forever, and then I'll get my cushy job, tra-la-la-la-la."

Hildegard put her hands over her ears. "Will you stop that? You have got to be the most annoying angel-in-training I have ever had the misfortune to meet."

"You're just saying that because you're jealous. My match is going to work and yours won't. And then I'm going to get a job in Relationship Division and be your boss."

"In your dreams! How did you ever make it into Heaven with that overblown ego of yours?"

Angelica lifted her chin, her pride coming to the fore. "It was probably my good works and exemplary behavior on Earth."

Her truth bracelet lit up, the siren blasting her ears. "Okay, okay. I got in on a clerical error. It wasn't my fault Sister Angelica and I arrived at the Pearly gates at the same time. The gatekeeper got us mixed up."

"Don't tell me they sent Sister Angelica to you-know-where?" Hildegard pointed downward in horror.

"No, thankfully St. Peter caught the error in time and rescued the sister. But by then I'd already spent some time here. St. Peter said it would be cruel to send me away after seeing all the wonders of Heaven."

"It's all beginning to make sense now," Hildegard said drily.

"Never mind about me. Aren't you excited about Riley and Iris?"

"They shared one bag of popcorn. So what? It's not like they made a lifetime pledge to each other."

"They're starting to like each other, Hildy. That's the important thing. Soon liking will turn to love and love will turn to commitment."

Angelica didn't have to be a mind reader to know that from the look on Hildy's face she thought so, too.

"Soon I'll get my wings and be a full-time employee in Relationship. Do you think I can get the really big wings?"

"Only Messengers and Avengers get those." Hildegard straightened her glasses. "Don't start counting your chickens just yet. You have to do more than match one mortal couple to earn your wings."

"Don't worry, I'll earn my wings. When I move into this office, I think I'm going to do some redecorating. How do you feel about lavender walls, Hildy?"

Hildegard sputtered for a few moments, too distracted by the thought of a purple office to remind Angelica not to call her Hildy.

Angelica considered that a very good sign.

Chapter Four

"Anybody home?"

Iris closed the front door with her hip while trying to balance several bags and boxes in her arms. Buddy greeted her, circling her in excitement and ferociously wagging his tail. Whiskers approached at a more leisurely pace, rubbing against Iris's legs as she placed the food she'd purchased in the tiny bar fridge.

"Big night, guys," she said to the animals. "Payday today. We're having actual food tonight. No more noodle soup."

She fed Buddy and Whiskers, and after drawing an X through the date on the calendar she'd pinned to the kitchen wall to mark off the days until her departure, she went upstairs to the bathroom to refill their water bowls. Some of her old optimism was returning. Since it had been payday today she'd not only been able to buy food, she also planned to give Riley a check for her first month's rent. Having a few dollars in her pocket made the world look a whole lot brighter.

She'd been living in Riley's house for a week and was grateful that so far nothing had gone up in smoke. For the last three days he'd been away on a training course but was due home any minute. She'd been surprised when he'd asked her to look after Buddy and the house in his absence and she was sure it hadn't been easy for him to entrust his precious home into her care. She just hoped he'd be okay with what she'd done while he was away.

Iris could hardly wait to see Riley. She'd been

surprised by how much she'd missed him. It didn't make any sense; she'd only known him a few days. Maybe she felt this way because he'd been so kind to her, taking her in the way he had. There was something so solid, so strong, so *real* about Riley.

She shook her head. If she didn't know better, she'd think she was falling for him or something.

Riley walked through the back door into the kitchen just as she entered with the water bowls. Iris's heart made a little pitter-pat in her chest at the sight of him. No man walked with as much innate grace as Riley did. For that matter, no man looked as good in his jeans as Riley either.

"Hi! How are you?" Iris asked.

Riley dropped his duffel bag near the back door and smiled. "Good. Glad to be home."

For a few moments they watched each other, neither speaking. Iris felt uncharacteristically shy, unable to do much more than stare like a love struck teenager.

Love struck?

She was saved from having to analyze that thought too deeply when Buddy raced to greet Riley as if he'd been gone a year instead of only three days. Iris enjoyed watching them roughhouse for a few minutes. It was obvious these two were crazy about each other. In Iris's books, anybody who loved animals was a fine, upstanding human.

"Thanks for looking after Buddy the last few days. I usually have to get somebody to feed him and walk him when I'm away."

"It was no trouble at all. Buddy and I are good friends now. Even Whiskers has made peace with him."

"I'm sure my drapes will be thankful. Aside from pet sitting, how was your week?"

"Very productive. I've got something for you." She pulled her rent check from the back pocket of her jeans. "Thank you for being so kind and waiting until I could pay you. I really appreciate it."

Riley grinned at the check and then stuck it in his pocket. "No problem. This is great. I'll put it toward my kitchen fund. A few more of these and I'll be able to afford a sink."

"A sink? What about the rest of the kitchen?"

"That might take a little longer."

"In that case, thank goodness for tiny fridges and microwaves," Iris said. "Speaking of tiny fridges, I have a surprise in there for you."

"Oh yeah? What kind of surprise?"

She opened the fridge door and took out the Styrofoam boxes of food. "Like I said, it was payday today so I went to the deli. I hope you like lasagna and salad. And I bought a bottle of wine, too."

"Wow, this is great. You didn't have to go to all this trouble."

"It was no trouble. I wanted to do it, partly because I'm sick of microwave popcorn and noodles, and partly because I wanted to show my appreciation. I don't know what I would have done if you hadn't taken me in."

"Renting the room to you is starting to look like one of the smartest things I've done lately," he said with a smile.

Without thinking she set the boxes on the fridge and took his hand. "I'm serious, Riley. I don't mind telling you how scared I was. Whiskers and I came very close to sleeping on a bench in the park with the other vagrants. So, thank you."

Riley gently brushed his fingers across her cheek, sending a rush of desire coursing through her body. "You're welcome. But I know you would have been okay, even if I hadn't rented you the room. You're a strong girl."

Iris didn't feel very strong at the moment. In fact, she felt as weak as a kitten, and just as vulnerable. She let go of Riley's hand and gave a shaky laugh.

"Yeah, that's me. Strong as a marshmallow." She picked up the boxes of food and turned away, afraid to look him in the eye and make a fool of herself.

"Hey, what's this?" Riley asked.

Iris turned to see him staring at her calendar. "That's just a little visual reminder for me. Only five more weeks until I hit the sunshine and you get rid of me."

Instead of laughing the way she thought he would, Riley continued to stare at the calendar.

"Right," he said. "Only five more weeks."

She wanted to ask him if he was okay, but something in his voice stopped her. Surely, he wouldn't miss her?

"Are you hungry?" she asked. Maybe he just needed to eat something. "I'm starved. I'll heat up the lasagna. Can you open the wine? It's in the bag on the floor. I even splurged on a corkscrew."

He smiled, seeming to shake off his unusual mood. "Smart girl. I usually buy the kind of wine that comes in a box."

While the lasagna reheated in the microwave, Riley gathered dishes and utensils from the box he kept next to the fridge. "Too bad we have to eat on the floor. This looks too nice to be roughing it."

"Actually we don't have to eat on the floor," Iris said. She suddenly felt very nervous about going into the dining room. "I got some of my furniture back. The sofa was too smoke-damaged to save, but the wooden table and chairs cleaned up fine. I put them in the dining room."

She followed him into the room, turning on the light over the table as he entered. Riley stopped dead in the middle of the room, clutching the wine and the dishes. He turned in a slow circle, looking all around him.

"What did you do?"

Not quite the reaction Iris had hoped for. "I did

it properly, honestly, just like you said you were going to do. I finished filling all the holes and then I sanded, primed, and painted. I just finished the second coat of paint last night." Her breath hitched a little. "Did I use the wrong colors? I thought those cans in the kitchen were the colors you wanted for the living room and dining room."

"The colors are perfect." He shook his head in wonder. "It looks beautiful. I can't believe you did all this."

Finally he turned to look at her. The expression on his face captured her. Iris had an overpowering urge to run into his arms and stay there for the rest of her life.

No! Was she crazy? In a few weeks time she'd be headed to her dream job as recreation director on a cruise ship. She was going to see a part of the world she'd never seen before. She was going to meet new, interesting people and have new, exciting experiences. She couldn't let herself be distracted now. Riley was a great guy but they were strictly landlord and tenant.

Weren't they?

"Why don't we eat?" Iris said, setting the food on the table. "I don't want it to get cold."

"Iris." Riley took her hand. "Thank you. I can't tell how much this means to me."

"You're welcome."

Iris couldn't breathe. Riley's green eyes were so warm, and so caring. His large hand engulfed hers, and made her feel very small but somehow very safe. She felt like they were in their own little world here in Riley's house.

He let go of her hand and turned away, and the spell was immediately broken. Iris breathed a relieved sigh. She wasn't sure what had come over her but she had to snap out of it.

Fast.

He reached into his pocket and pulled out her

check. He handed it to her. "Under the circumstances, I can't take this from you."

"No, don't be silly. Keep it."

"Iris, after all the work you did, it's too much."

She wanted him to have the money. It was obvious he needed it to finish the work on the house. After all, he'd only rented her the room for the money.

"I'll make you a deal," she said. "You keep the money. Tomorrow you can buy food at the deli. A girl's gotta eat, you know."

Riley looked as if he wanted to argue, but at last he shook his head and smiled. She caught a glimpse of a dimple in his cheek.

"Okay. You've got a deal. I'll make sure you eat properly."

"Now, if this discussion is over, can we have dinner?"

"Of course."

Riley set the table with the mismatched plates and cutlery. They drank their wine from plastic glasses decorated with happy faces. Somehow it seemed appropriate.

"I'd like to make a toast," he said, raising his happy-face glass to her. "To good food and wine, and to new friends."

Iris touched her glass to his. "To new friends."

"I don't believe it. Look." Riley pointed across the room

Iris followed his gaze. Buddy was sleeping in his bed in a corner of the living room. Whiskers snuggled in close beside him, her head resting on his paw. Buddy woke up long enough to give her head a couple of licks and then went back to sleep.

"They've been doing that for the last couple of days," Iris said. "I think it's cute."

Riley shook his head. "Remarkable. I thought they were going to rip each other to shreds at one point."

"Once they got over the initial shock, I guess they decided they liked each other."

Sort of like us. Iris took a fortifying sip of wine. "Riley, I know this is a lot to ask, but since Buddy and Whiskers seem to get along so well now, would you consider keeping her when I go? I haven't been able to find a good home for her and I can't bear the thought of having to surrender her to the Humane Society." Her inability to find a home for Whiskers had been weighing on her for some time.

Riley looked at her in surprise. "I've never really thought of myself as a cat person, but I guess as long as Buddy's happy with the arrangement, I can take her in."

Iris nearly cried in relief. "Thank you, Riley. I can't tell you how much this means to me. How can I ever repay you?"

As she said the words, visions of tumbled sheets and warm skin over hard muscle popped into Iris's brain. Her face heated with embarrassment. Was she seriously thinking about repaying him with sex? Where had that come from?

"I'll look after her, Iris. Don't worry."

They ate the rest of their meal in silence. When they were done, Riley poured them each another glass of wine, and then leaned back in his chair and looked around.

"I'm still amazed by what you accomplished here in such a short time. It's starting to actually look like a house, except for the whole no kitchen thing."

"You've done a beautiful job restoring the woodwork around the doors and windows. Once these floors are redone, these two rooms are going to look like a million bucks."

"I wish I could finish the whole thing right now but I'm totally tapped out. Before I could even start on any of the cosmetic stuff I had to put on a new roof, install new wiring and plumbing, and shore up the foundation. That didn't leave much money for anything else."

"You'll finish all the work someday. It's a labor of love for you."

Riley grinned. "Yeah, I guess it is. There's something really satisfying about bringing this old house back to life."

"I know what you mean," Iris said. "I felt the same way when I was painting. It was like I was taking something that was broken and ugly and making it beautiful again."

To Iris's amazement she'd actually enjoyed painting and discovered she was quite good at it. She almost wished she could get her hands on another project.

"Yeah, that's exactly what I mean." He looked a little sheepish. "This is going to sound kind of crazy but I feel like the house is pleased I'm looking after her. She was neglected for a long time."

"It doesn't sound crazy at all," Iris said. "It sounds like you're a person who takes care of the things you love."

As she gazed into Riley's eyes, currents of awareness flowed between them. Iris's heart beat wildly and she couldn't seem to get enough air into her lungs. It was all she could do not to reach out to touch his hand again.

Finally, she looked away, forcing herself to laugh.

"This old house is almost human. She's a little temperamental, a little vain. But I think she's willing to go through the pain of reconstructive surgery if it means she'll be young and beautiful again. She reminds me of my grandmother from Boston."

Riley laughed, the sound deep and rich and happy. "Your grandmother?"

"Yeah. She hated looking old. When she was in her sixties she had a face-lift. It didn't really make her look any younger, just perennially surprised."

"What's her name?"

"Betty. Why?"

Riley lifted his wine glass and looked around the room. "I christen thee Betty, O vain house, and solemnly promise to care and beautify you for the rest of my natural life. Because I'll probably be paying through the nose for you for the rest of my natural life."

Iris laughed, charmed by Riley's quirky sense of humor. She lifted her plastic glass and touched his. "To Betty."

"To Betty."

As Iris drank the rest of her wine, a pang of regret settled on her heart. She'd never see Betty completely restored and would no longer be a part of her rehabilitation. The thought saddened her far more than she'd ever thought possible.

****

"Ah, that's so cute. Iris is falling in love."

Hildegard crossed her arms, a sour look on her face. "Do you mean she's falling in love with Riley or with Betty?"

"Both!" Angelica laughed and clapped her hands. "Don't you see Hildy? If she loves Betty as much as Riley does, there's no way she's going to want to leave. You're just jealous because my match is working."

"Maybe," Hildegard conceded. "But I really do want what's best for both Iris and Riley. What if throwing them together just makes them unhappy?"

"How could that be possible?"

"If Iris decides to leave, regardless of her feelings for Riley, it's going to break his heart. And hers."

Angelica had to admit Hildy had a point. What if Iris decided to stay with Riley, but then felt as if she'd missed the opportunity of her life by not taking the cruise ship job? She'd be miserable and so would he. Angelica truly cared about Iris and Riley and wanted them to be happy. Together.

But she wasn't about to let Hildy know she had doubts.

"Too late," Hildegard said with a grin. "Mind reading angel here, remember?"

"Oh, fiddlesticks."

"And don't call me Hildy."

Chapter Five

"There's no way the Trailblazers should have lost the game."

"You've got to admit, Riley, the Suns totally outplayed them."

"I suppose. They need some scoring out of their big guns."

Riley and Iris debated the basketball game all the way home, first on the train and then on the walk to the house. Iris's intimate knowledge of the game, not to mention her passion, amazed him. When she'd received a couple of free tickets from a client and invited him along, Riley thought he'd have to spend the afternoon explaining the rules of the game to her. Far from it. Iris knew the game, the players, the coaches, and even the history. Just one more thing they had in common.

She's leaving me in three weeks.

Riley tried to push the thought away, unwilling to consider the prospect. He hated the damn calendar she kept in the kitchen. It mocked him, telling him every day that she'd soon be leaving him. He felt as if he'd known Iris for years, that she'd always been a part of his life. The thought of her going away, and the idea that he might never see her again, caused an ache in his chest.

"Are you all right?" Iris asked.

Riley forced himself back to the present. "I'm fine. Why?"

"You've got a funny look on your face, like you're in pain or something."

"Maybe a little indigestion," he lied. "Too many

hot dogs."

She touched his arm. "I've got ginger ale at home. It might make you feel better."

Riley glanced at her as they walked. God, she was sweet. He was even starting to like the blue streak in her hair.

"Thanks," he said. "I'll be fine."

A big black Cadillac was parked at the curb in front of his house. Riley's jaw clenched. What the hell did Joe Gardiner want?

Iris slipped her hand into his and Riley held it tightly.

"Don't worry. He can't do anything to you anymore."

As they approached the house Joe Gardiner got out of his car.

"Well, if it isn't my two favorite people," he said.

"What do you want, Gardiner?"

"I'm looking to buy property in this neighborhood, Mr. Benson. Your next door neighbor is thinking about selling."

Riley's next door neighbor was Mrs. Parker, a widow in her sixties. He knew her home was too big for her, now that her husband was gone and her children had moved away. It was also her only financial asset. Gardiner would try to pick it up for a song, like he did with Aunt Molly and Uncle Claude's house. As far as he knew, Mrs. Parker hadn't put her house on the market. How did Gardiner know she was thinking of selling? The man could smell fresh blood like a shark. Riley made a mental note to speak to Mrs. Parker.

Gardiner examined the outside of Riley's house. Riley knew what he saw. Aside from the new roof, he hadn't had the time or the money to make any changes to the exterior. The paint was peeling, and the front porch was rotting into the ground. The sidewalk was cracked and heaving and the lawn in the front yard was mostly non-existent. When the foundation work had been done, the contractor had had to dig a trench all around the house, destroying the flower beds and roses his Aunt Molly had tended so carefully. Molly probably looked down from Heaven every day with a tear in her eye.

"It looks like you still have plenty of work to do on your house," Gardiner said, a cocky smile on his face. "An old place like this can be quite a money pit. I'd be happy to take it off your hands. You should consider it."

"I'll consider it. Right after Hell freezes over."

The smile left Gardiner's face. "If I decide to call in my loan you won't have any choice but to sell to me. Maybe you should consider that." He leered at Iris, looking her up and down. "If she's living with you, there probably won't be anything left of the house soon anyway. I hope screwing her is worth the financial disaster."

A red haze of anger formed in front of Riley's eyes. He lunged at Gardiner and grabbed him by his shirt collar, intent on wiping the arrogant smirk from his face.

"Riley, no! He isn't worth it," Iris shouted.

Beads of sweat formed on Gardiner's brow. The urge to ram his fist into the bastard's soft belly nearly overwhelmed Riley. He felt Iris's hand on his arm.

"Please, don't," she whispered. "Let him go."

The anxiety in her voice broke through his anger. The last thing he wanted was to upset Iris by beating Gardiner to a pulp. He pushed Gardiner hard against the Cadillac and dropped his hands from his shirt.

"Get out of here and don't ever let me see you in this neighborhood again."

Gardiner scrambled around the car and opened the driver's side door.

"You two deserve each other! You're both crazy!"

He jumped into his Cadillac and sped off down

the street. Riley watched him go, anger still vibrating through him. The bastard. Nobody talked like that about Iris and got away with it.

Iris tugged gently on his arm. "Let's go inside."

Riley released a pent-up breath and let her lead him into the house.

"What did Gardiner mean about calling your loan in?"

"It's nothing, Iris. Don't worry about it."

"I think I've earned the right to know what's going on."

Her quiet dignity in the face of Gardiner's crude insults only made him admire her more. And she was right. She had earned the right to know.

"I'll make some tea and tell you about it."

"Okay."

By the time Riley finished making tea, he had calmed down. He brought the pot of herbal tea to the dining room table where Iris waited for him.

She sipped her tea, but said nothing, giving him the chance to collect his thoughts. Riley toyed with his cup.

"I told you about my great aunt and uncle raising me in this house after my parents died."

Iris nodded.

"When Gardiner stole the house from them, I swore I'd get it back some day. Finally, he was ready to sell it to me. I was thrilled."

"Why do I sense a big 'but' coming?"

Riley grinned ruefully. "I guess you could say that. Gardiner knew how much I wanted this property. He threatened to demolish the house if I didn't pay him what he wanted."

"My God, Riley, that's extortion. How did he get away with it?"

"Probably because I let him. I knew he would do it. The house had lots of problems, a leaking roof, and a crumbling foundation. He even got a demolition permit from the city. So I agreed to his terms."

"His terms?"

"He asked an exorbitant amount of money for the house, way more than it was worth. I could only secure a portion of the mortgage from the bank. The rest I had to borrow from him and he's been holding it over my head ever since."

"That's got to be illegal. At the very least it's unethical. Why didn't you go to the police or a lawyer or something?"

"Before I got the house I was afraid to complain to anyone because I knew he'd tear the house down. And since I moved in I just don't have the time or the money to hire a lawyer. Every spare dollar and extra minute I have goes into this house."

Agitated, Riley got to his feet. He shook his head and laughed but he wasn't feeling very jovial.

"Maybe Gardiner is right. Maybe I should sell it back to him. The place is wearing me down."

"You can't do that, Riley," Iris protested. She rose as well, stepping around the table to stand in front of him and reach for his hand. "This is Betty, remember? She needs you, and you need her. You two belong together."

"Till death do us part?"

She laughed and squeezed his hand. "Let's hope it doesn't come to that."

Riley looked into her beautiful blue eyes and her smiling face and did the only thing he was capable of doing at the moment.

He kissed her.

Maybe later, he told himself, when sanity returned, he'd think of a hundred reasons why pulling Iris into his arms, holding her snug against his body, and plundering her soft, sweet mouth was not a good idea. But for now, right now, as she wound her arms around his neck and made tiny sounds of excitement deep in her throat, it felt exactly right.

Riley cupped her bottom and pulled her against his erection. *Heaven.* Having Iris in his corner made him believe everything was possible.

He stepped backward toward the stairs, pulling Iris with him, intent on taking her upstairs to his room. He suddenly tripped, nearly losing his balance. He glanced behind him and saw the object he'd stumbled over. A set of luggage sat next to the stairs, still bearing tags from the retailer.

"What the hell is this?"

Iris kissed his neck. "I'm sorry. I should have taken them up to my room."

Iris had bought new luggage for her trip. Her plans hadn't changed.

She's leaving me.

The thought acted as effectively as a bucket of cold water tossed over his head. What was he doing? She was leaving in three weeks and didn't plan to return. The calendar in the kitchen reminded him of that every day. Why start something that would only lead to heartache?

He pulled back from Iris, gently disengaging her arms from his neck. At first her passion-filled eyes registered confusion, and then gradually, as realization dawned, he saw hurt flicker in their blue depths. Riley never imagined that causing pain to Iris could nearly bring him to his knees and destroy his resolve.

Why couldn't they take pleasure in each other for the next three weeks? Why should they deny themselves what Riley knew would be the best sex of their lives? Why was he throwing it all away?

Because he'd already lost too many people in his life.

And Riley instinctively knew that if he let himself get close to Iris, let himself love her, a part of him would not survive when she left.

"Iris, I'm sorry."

She touched her hand to her forehead, her eyes

still dazed. "No, there's nothing to be sorry for. We're both adults."

Her pain sliced through him. "Iris—"

"No." She put her finger to his lips, her eyes shining with unshed tears. "No, don't say anything. It's all right, really."

She stepped away. "It's getting late. I'm going upstairs. Goodnight Riley."

"Goodnight."

He watched her hurry from the room, his heart heavy. Maybe it was already too late to avoid heartache.

Perhaps it had been too late the moment he'd met her.

****

"Why do mortals have to be so complicated?" Angelica moaned. "Iris is right there in front of him. She's kissing him for Heaven's sake! Can't he see she's his soul mate?"

Hildegard sighed. "Now you know the frustrations of this job. It's not always as obvious to mortals as it is to us who the right match for them is. Old hurts and childhood traumas can make it difficult for mortals to trust."

Angelica flopped into Hildy's office chair. "This is so frustrating. It would be so much easier if we could speak to them in person, explain things to them—"

"No! Absolutely not! You know the rules, Angelica. Don't even think about breaking them."

"Hildy, don't you see? They're going to throw away their chance for true happiness."

"Patience, angel-in-training. Give them some time to turn things around. And if they don't, then it's not meant to be."

The thought depressed Angelica. It *was* meant to be. She could feel it to the tips of her toes. If only she could talk to them—

"Angelica!"

"Okay, okay."

She toyed with the bugle beads on her gown. "I hate sitting around waiting like this. Can we at least do something to that awful Joe Gardiner? How about zapping him with a bolt of lightning?"

"We're not allowed to do stuff like that. Unfortunately. But we can report him to Avenger Division. They can make his life a living you-know-what in the afterlife."

"Oh, I like it when you talk revenge."

Hildegard adjusted her glasses. "It's not revenge, Angelica. That's not what we're about. It's all about justice. Sometimes mortals don't get proper justice on Earth, but angels always make sure they receive it in the afterlife."

"Gosh, we're noble," Angelica said. "I've never thought of myself as being so magnanimous and wonderful before."

Hildegard rolled her eyes. "Get over yourself. We'll let Avenger Division take care of Joe Gardiner. You and I have bigger concerns."

"What do you mean?"

"There's only three weeks left. How is Riley going to convince Iris to stay? And how is Iris going to convince Riley that she's got staying power?"

"Does this mean you think Iris and Riley are soul mates, that they should be together?"

"Maybe."

"And does this mean I'll soon be working here with you in Relationship Division?"

"I'm not making any promises. Besides, Antonio is still waiting in the wings."

"You know as well as I do that now that she's met Riley she won't be interested in anyone else," Angelica said. "I'm afraid it's either Riley or no one for Iris."

Hildegard sighed. "I'm afraid you're right."

Chapter Six

Iris stuck her head through the door of the sunroom at the back of the house where Riley was replacing some of the floor boards. "Riley, can you come with me for a minute? There's someone here I'd like you to meet."

Riley set down his hammer and got to his feet. "Who's that?"

"A friend of mine," Iris said. She hoped Riley wouldn't be angry she'd told his story to someone else. But if Nathan was able to help him, it would be worth it even if Riley wasn't pleased with her meddling.

Iris led Riley into the living room where her friend waited. "Riley, this is Nathan Jarvis. He's a client of mine, and a friend. I've helped Nathan and his wife Jill plan several of their holidays. Nathan, this is my landlord, Riley Benson."

"This young lady is a marvel," Nathan said as he shook Riley's hand. "I've never met a travel agent who does more research on the places she sends us or who cares more about our enjoyment on our trips."

"That sounds like Iris." Riley grinned at her with what felt to Iris like pride. Her heart expanded in her chest.

"I've told you before, Iris," Nathan said, "anytime you want to set up your own travel agency you let me know. I'll back you one hundred percent."

"I'm not sure I'm ready to go out on my own, but thank you for the offer. You know how much your support means to me. But like I told you earlier, there is something I'm hoping you can help us with."

Iris turned to Riley. "Nathan is one of the best lawyers in the city. I told him about your situation with Joe Gardiner."

Riley glanced at Nathan and then back at Iris. "I wish you hadn't done that."

"Iris was right to come to me," Nathan said. "From what she told me, the contract you entered into with Gardiner was made under duress. It might even be argued that extortion is involved. I'd like to go over any documents you have and hear your statement so I know if we have a case."

"Look, Mr. Jarvis, I appreciate your interest, but I can't possibly pay your fees, whatever they are."

Nathan grinned. "It's true, Mr. Benson. I don't come cheap. I'm offering my services to you *gratis* because Iris is a friend of mine and she seems to think you're worth the effort."

"Please Riley, talk to Nathan. Maybe there's a legal way out of the terrible contract you made with Gardiner." She couldn't leave in another three weeks knowing that Gardiner was holding a gun to Riley's head.

Riley turned to Nathan. "You really think there's a possibility I could get out of this contract?"

"I'd have to do more research, but from what I've heard so far, I'd say there was a very good possibility."

Riley took Iris's hand and gave it a squeeze. His beautiful eyes looked deeply into hers. Iris trembled from head to toe. She wanted to step into his arms, wrap herself around him, and never let him go. She contented herself by squeezing his hand in return.

Eventually Riley tore his gaze away from Iris and turned his attention back to Nathan. "Okay, Mr. Jarvis—Nathan. Why don't we have a seat at the dining room table and I'll tell you everything I know."

"I'll make us some sandwiches," Iris said. "This

might take a while."

A huge rush of relief flowed through her. Riley was getting the help he needed with his legal problems. In addition, she'd been speaking with a friend who was looking for a place to live. With any luck she'd soon have a new tenant lined up for him, someone to help offset the costs of renovating Betty. She'd even spoken to another client, a landscape designer, who offered to do the landscaping of the house at cost. By the time she left, Riley would be well on his way to making his dream of bringing Betty back to life come true.

By the time I leave...

The prospect of jetting off to the Mediterranean now felt like a burdensome obligation rather than the exciting opportunity it had once been. Iris shook her head as she buttered bread and spread cold cuts. She'd planned this adventure for months. She wanted to see the world.

But everything was different now.

When Riley kissed her three nights ago Iris's world tipped on its axis. His kiss awakened a longing inside her soul and she knew without any doubt that she loved him. In that one wonderful, brief kiss, she'd found her life's purpose. She was meant to spend her life with Riley, living and loving in this house.

There was only one problem with that scenario. Riley didn't feel the same way.

Maybe she could convince him somehow. Maybe if he kissed her again he'd realize they belonged together. Maybe then he'd ask her to stay.

And maybe pigs could fly.

Iris cut the sandwiches in quarters and sighed. Once or twice she'd caught him staring at her with an odd expression, and sometimes his hand would linger on hers as if he enjoyed touching her. These occasions gave her hope that in time Riley would learn to care for her.

But time was something she had very little of. Three more weeks and the cruise began.

She couldn't make Riley love her. If he didn't feel the same way she did, she couldn't force the emotion from him. Unless he asked her to stay, she'd leave the way she'd originally planned.

Tears welled in her eyes and she had to cover her mouth to muffle her sob. There had to be another way!

She gathered her emotions and wiped her eyes before bringing the tray of sandwiches into the dining room. She forced herself to make small talk and to listen to the conversation, but all the while she wanted to retreat into her room and cry.

Several hours, and many cups of tea later, Nathan packed his briefcase and left, promising to look into the matter further and get back to them soon. Iris loaded cups and plates into the basin they used to wash dishes. Riley took the basin from her and set it on the kitchen floor.

"Leave it, Iris. I'd like to talk to you."

"Are you angry I went behind your back to talk to Nathan?"

"You should have told me what you planned to do, but no, I'm not angry with you." He took her hands in his. "It's a relief to know there's a light at the end of the tunnel I've been in. And it's a comfort to know I'm not alone in the tunnel. Thank you."

"You're welcome," she whispered.

Iris's heart fluttered as Riley closed the distance between them. Inch by excruciating inch, he lowered his head to hers, and Iris held her breath, her body shuddering in delicious anticipation as she waited for his kiss. When his lips finally touched hers, a dam burst open, releasing a torrent of emotions long held back. Iris wound her arms around his neck, holding him tightly, melding her body to his. He tasted sweet, like the honey he used in his tea. She breathed in his unique scent, a combination of spicy aftershave and hardworking male. She never wanted to let him go.

Riley abruptly broke the kiss. Shock and something that looked like fear filled his eyes.

"I hadn't meant to do that. I'm sorry."

"Are you sorry you kissed me?" she whispered.

Riley averted his gaze and shook his head slightly. But the look on his face was so remorseful that Iris knew she had her answer.

He was sorry.

He took several steps away from her. She wrapped her arms around herself, feeling suddenly cold.

"We can't let this happen again," he said. "There's no point."

Did he mean because she was leaving or because he didn't care about her?

"I start a four-day shift early tomorrow morning," Riley said, not quite looking at her. "I should get some sleep."

"Yes, of course."

"I probably won't see you much the next few days." He stood in front of her but Iris knew he'd already left her.

Iris swallowed. "No, probably not."

For a moment he looked as if he wanted to say more. Instead, he nodded briskly.

"Goodnight."

"Goodnight."

Iris watched him leave the kitchen and hurry up the stairs. She heard the soft click of his bedroom door closing.

The exact same sound her heart made as it broke in two.

The phone rang, jolting her from her thoughts. She took a deep breath and picked up the cordless phone, the only one in the house, from its base on top of the fridge. Her hand trembled as she gripped the phone.

"Hello?"

"Ms. Jennings? This is Abby Keyser with Columbus Cruise Lines. I'm sorry to be calling so late, but something's come up and I need to speak with you. I tried calling your cell phone but couldn't get through. Thank goodness you emailed me your new home number."

Ms. Keyser's inability to reach her on her cell phone didn't surprise Iris since she no longer had a cell phone. She'd given it up after she'd made her settlement with Gardiner and had no money left for extras. Iris massaged her temple, not wanting to think about the cruise right now.

"It *is* late, Ms. Keyser. Maybe you can call tomorrow."

"I'm sorry, but it's imperative we speak now. We've added an additional week-long cruise to the beginning of the season because we've received so much demand. We wonder if you could start two weeks earlier than we'd originally planned."

"Two weeks earlier?" Iris's brain whirled. "That would mean I'd have to leave Portland by the end of this week."

"Yes, that's right. Would you be able to rearrange your schedule? We would take care of your flight to Athens."

I'd have to leave Riley two weeks earlier.

"I...I don't know," she stalled. "I'd have to speak to my employer. I don't want to leave her or my clients in the lurch. Can I call you back tomorrow?"

"Yes, of course." Ms. Keyser gave Iris her number. "Please contact me as soon as possible."

Iris stood in the middle of the living room staring at the pretty blue-green walls for a long time after she hung up the phone. She remembered how much fun she'd had painting them, and how thrilled she'd been with Riley's reaction. The last few weeks her world had revolved around Riley and his happiness. She'd let herself care for him more than any man she'd ever known, had let herself fall in love with him. But he'd just made it abundantly clear once again that he didn't share her feelings.

Maybe a quick and fast break was for the best. Staying on in Riley's house would only make her wish for things that could never be. She'd make the arrangements tomorrow after she'd spoken to her boss. It was the right thing to do.

But if it was so right, why did she feel so completely miserable?

****

Angelica blew her nose into a cloth hankie. "Don't go, Iris, don't go! Oh, poor Iris. She's in love with Riley. Why can't she tell him how she feels? Why do mortals have to be so blind to love?"

Hildegard patted her back. "I suppose she can't tell him how she feels because she's afraid he doesn't feel the same way. She's afraid of being hurt."

"We have to do something quick, Hildy, before Iris leaves. We can't let them walk away from each other. They're soul mates, for goodness sake! Don't they know that?"

"We have to let them make their own decisions, Angelica. Even if they're bad ones. Mortals have free will, remember?"

"Oh phooey on free will! Mortals would be a lot happier if they just listened to us angels."

Hildegard chuckled. "I can't say I disagree with you."

Angelica grabbed Hildegard's arm. "Then help me go to Earth. I don't care about the rules and the trouble I'll get into. I've got to save them."

"No you can't! You could get kicked out of Heaven for disobedience." She straightened her tweed jacket. "I'll do it."

"What? You? What about following all the rules? You're the one who told me—"

"I know what I told you. Rules are important, but sometimes breaking them to achieve a greater good is even more important. I'm going to Earth to deal with Riley and Iris."

"No! You can't go! You'll get into trouble. I'm just a lowly angel-in-training with nothing to lose. You're somebody here in Heaven, Hildy. If anyone should risk going to Earth to talk some sense into those two, it should be me."

"But I know how to avoid security better than you do. And besides, you are someone in Heaven. You're Angelica and you're as important as anyone else."

"Oh, Hildy." Angelica fanned her hand in front of her face. "You're going to make me cry again."

Hildegard handed her another hankie. "Here. Cry all you want."

"No," Angelica said, carefully dabbing her eyes. "I don't want my mascara to run."

"Perish the thought."

"We'll both go," Angelica said once her eyes were dry. She checked her compact mirror to make sure her mascara was still in place. "I'll take Iris and you take Riley. We'll give them a little talking-to. We're in, we're out, problem solved."

"I hope so." Hildegard frowned. "Mortals are notoriously fickle. They say they're doing one thing and then turn around and do exactly the opposite."

"Let's hope that doesn't happen," Angelica said. "So how do we get to Earth from here?"

"First I dial in Iris and Riley's coordinates into my handheld locating system." She adjusted some dials and hit a few keys on her small locater. "It's supposed to be used for getting around the vast distances in Heaven, but in a pinch it can be used to travel to Earth, although I've never tried it before. Now, we've only got a short amount of time before someone figures out we've flown the coop. We have to convince Riley and Iris they love each other and want to be together forever and get back here before we're missed."

"Okay. I'll be fast. Won't Iris and Riley be shocked to get a call from angels? Won't we freak them out?"

"Maybe, but the memory of our visit won't stay with them. It will quickly fade until it disappears completely. But they will always remember our conversation."

"That sounds great. What do we do now?"

"We do this."

Hildegard hit the enter button on her locater and they both disappeared in a puff of smoke.

Chapter Seven

Iris couldn't concentrate. She stared at her computer monitor but all she could see was Riley's face. She hadn't even left and she missed him already.

"You were telling me about Paris," her client said, bringing her back to the present. Her client sat on the other side of her desk and smiled, her blonde curls bouncing and rings shining on every manicured finger.

"Yes, Paris. The City of Lights. It's probably the most romantic city in the world." The thought depressed Iris.

"A city made for lovers." The woman's large blue eyes sparkled with flashes of light. The woman's eyes actually *were* sparkling. Iris sat back in her chair and rubbed her tired eyes. She'd been spending way too much time in front of the computer.

"I think Paris would be a perfect place for a honeymoon, don't you?"

Iris could imagine it perfectly. Walking along the Seine, drinking coffee in a sidewalk café, having a quiet glass of wine at an intimate restaurant. She could see the pictures in her mind so clearly. And in every picture Riley was at her side.

Iris shook her head to dispel the images. What was the matter with her? She was never going on a honeymoon with Riley. She was leaving Portland forever in five days. She'd made all the arrangements.

"Would you like me to make some bookings in Paris for you?" she asked her client. What was the woman's name again? Had she told her?

The woman just smiled. "Paris in springtime is the perfect place for lovers. Everything is fresh and new and full of promise."

"Yes." The images raced through her head once more. This time she and Riley strolled hand in hand through a park, cherry blossoms falling like fragrant flakes of snow. He looked at her with adoration.

Why was she torturing herself like this? Riley didn't love her and never would.

Iris burst into tears. Not quiet weeping but big wrenching sobs complete with hysterical hiccups and a runny nose. She covered her mouth in mortification.

"I'm sorry," she said, reaching for a tissue. "I don't know what came over me. You must think I'm crazy."

"No Iris, I don't think you're crazy. I think you're in love." The woman smiled kindly, her blonde curls bouncing once more as she tipped her head to one side. "The sooner you do something about it, the better you'll feel."

Iris stared at her, confused. How did this woman know how she felt? Did she have a stamp on her forehead declaring her feelings, *Victim of Unrequited Love*? She felt foggy-brained, as if half asleep. Was she dreaming and just didn't realize it? Iris shaded her eyes with her hand, blinded by a bright light. Was the woman glowing?

The woman took her hand. Warmth emanated from Iris's fingertips all the way up her arm. Sudden fear stole her breath. What was happening to her?

"You don't need to be afraid of anything, Iris. Not of me and not of your feelings for Riley. Tell him how you feel. Tell him you love him. You belong together. You're soul mates."

Suddenly it was all so clear. She loved him and she needed to let him know.

She needed to be with him.

"Yes, I have to tell him I love him."

The woman squeezed her hand. "Good. My work is done."

Iris blinked and when she opened her eyes once more the woman with the blonde curly hair had disappeared. Around her the other agents carried on with their work as if nothing out of the ordinary had happened. Perhaps she'd dreamed the blonde woman. Or maybe she'd lost her mind.

But one thing had certainly changed. She couldn't walk away from Riley. She wanted to spend the rest of her life with him. She loved him.

Iris couldn't wait to tell him.

****

"Hey, Riley!"

Riley's head swiveled at his friend Frank's shout. Frank waved him over. "There's a lady here to see you."

Riley's heart beat faster. *Iris.* She'd come to see him.

But when he raced down the stairs into the common area, he was disheartened to find a middle-aged woman in a tweed suit polishing her steel framed glasses. He did his best to disguise his disappointment.

"I understand you were looking for me."

"Yes, I'm with Nathan Jarvis's office," she said. "We wanted to let you know Mr. Jarvis has done some research and believes you have a good case against Mr. Gardiner. Mr. Jarvis is also notifying the authorities about the situation. There's a possibility they will charge Mr. Gardiner with extortion."

"That's wonderful news. Thank you for telling me." He couldn't wait to tell Iris.

"Yes, you should tell Iris. If she hadn't contacted Mr. Jarvis you would have been indebted to Mr. Gardiner forever."

Riley stepped back, alarmed. "How did you know

I was thinking about Iris?"

She smiled. "You're always thinking about Iris, aren't you, Riley? She means everything to you."

The woman's eyes looked so kind, even behind her thick glasses. He felt like he could talk to her.

"Yes, she means everything to me."

"You're in love with her."

"Yes, I'm in love with her." The room swayed a little and he had to sit in one of the chairs. It was the first time he'd admitted to anyone, including himself, that he loved Iris.

"Why don't you tell her?" she asked.

Riley shook his head. "I can't. I'm afraid."

"What are you afraid of Riley?"

"I'm afraid I'll lose her." A part of Riley couldn't believe he was saying these things to a perfect stranger, that they were pouring out of him. But another part of him was hugely relieved to admit how he felt.

"Why do you think you'll lose her?"

"Because I've lost everyone I've ever loved. My parents, my Aunt Molly and Uncle Claude. Iris practically has one foot out the door already. I can't bear to lose anyone else. Maybe it's better to be alone."

"It's never better to be alone, Riley. Love is always worth the risk. Tell her you love her, fight for her. If you don't, she's going to leave and never know how you feel."

"I love her. I really love her."

"Tell her, Riley."

"I will."

The woman smiled. She straightened her tweed jacket. "Good. I should be going now. Goodbye. Don't forget our conversation. At least for now."

And then she was gone. Riley blinked a couple of times. Where did she go? Had he actually seen her leave the fire hall?

It didn't matter. What was important was that

he loved Iris. He couldn't let her leave him. He needed her here with him forever. If he had to beg her to stay then that's what he'd do.

Riley ran back upstairs. "Frank, can you do me a favor?"

"What's that?"

"Can you find someone to cover the rest of my shift? I've got to get home."

"Is it an emergency?"

Riley nodded grimly. "Absolutely. My whole future is at stake."

****

Iris sat on the edge of her bed, the cordless phone trembling in her hands. Whiskers curled up next to her and Buddy sat at her feet with his head in her lap, looking up at her with soulful eyes. Both animals sensed her nervousness. She was about to tell Riley she loved him.

She punched in the number of Riley's fire hall before she could lose her nerve. A deep male voice answered after a couple of rings.

"Hello?"

"Hello, can I speak to Riley Benson, please."

"I'm sorry. He's not here. He had an emergency at home. He left early."

An emergency at home? I'm the only one having an emergency at home. "Oh. Thank you. Goodbye."

Iris hung her head. What did she do now? It had taken every ounce of courage she possessed to call the fire hall. Where could he be? And why would he lie about an emergency at home?

Iris began to pace her small room. Buddy fell into step beside her and Whiskers watched from the bed. She wanted to spend the rest of her life with Riley, but what if he didn't feel the same way? What if all the feelings were strictly on her side? What if the woman in her crazy dream had been totally wrong about Riley being her soul mate?

Oh, Lord. She was in serious trouble. She was

actually starting to believe her own hallucinations.

Iris flopped onto her bed, holding her head in her hands. Lost in her own thoughts, she barely noticed when Buddy emitted a sharp bark and left the room.

What was she going to do? The idea of leaving on the cruise, of leaving Riley, tore her heart to shreds, but the thought of staying, knowing he didn't love her, hurt even more. She curled into a fetal position and moaned.

"Iris? Sweetheart, what's wrong? Are you okay?"

The next thing Iris knew she was in Riley's lap, her head resting against his broad chest. He kissed her hair and whispered reassurances to her.

"The guy at the fire hall told me you had an emergency," she sniffed.

Riley went very still. "You phoned the fire hall?"

"Yes. What was the emergency?"

"I forgot to tell you something."

She lifted her head to look at him. "You did? What?"

He swallowed, uncertainty clouding his eyes. "I forgot to tell you I love you."

For a second she stared at him, his words taking a moment to register. Then she smiled, her heart expanding with happiness.

He loves me!

"I love you, too."

Joy filled her, cramming every little nook and cranny of her soul, plugging all the empty spots until she could barely stand so much bliss.

She wound her arms around his neck and kissed him, trying to pour all the love she felt for him into her kiss. It was Heaven to touch him, to run her hands over his muscular back, to drink in the clean, male scent of him.

Riley broke the kiss and rested his forehead against hers. He held her close, his breathing uneven. "You mean it?"

The hope glimmering in the green depths of his eyes was tempered with caution. She wanted him to have no misgivings, no doubts about the way she felt. She gently caressed his face and smiled into his eyes.

"Yes, I really mean it. I love you, Riley. Like crazy."

He grinned, the doubt in his eyes evaporating like dew in the morning sunshine.

"I'm pretty crazy about you myself."

He tightened his hold on her, trailing urgent kisses along her jawline and on the sensitive skin behind her ear.

"Iris, do you have any idea what you do to me? What you've been doing to me the last few weeks?"

Kissing the corner of his mouth, Iris smoothed her hands over his hair, loving the silky feel of it.

"Hmmm. Tell me all about it."

Riley's expression was fierce. He held her face between his hands.

"I love you, Iris."

"I love you, too."

He kissed her with such tenderness it brought tears to Iris's eyes. She'd never forget this moment and the look on his face as long as she lived.

A sharp bark followed by a high-pitched whine diverted their attention. Buddy peered at them over the edge of the bed, his dark eyes glistening. Whiskers watched them from her perch on top of the dresser.

"I think we've got an audience," Riley said.

"You think they approve?"

"I think they're probably saying, 'What took you so long?' "

Iris shifted in his lap to straddle him, her hands restlessly exploring his muscled back and arms. "I'm starting to feel pretty impatient myself."

Riley chuckled as he tugged her T-shirt over her head. "Don't worry, sweetheart. Your wait is over."

****

Hildegard closed the Earth window with a snap of her fingers. Angelica turned to her.

"What did you do that for? We were just getting to the best part."

"Iris and Riley deserve some privacy. Besides, we're angels, not voyeurs."

"I suppose you're right," Angelica sighed.

"Cheer up, angel-in-training. We've done what we set out to do."

"We did, didn't we? We made them fall in love! We should celebrate. I believe a new outfit is in order!"

"A new outfit? You've already got more clothes than ten angels put together. Why would you need more?"

"Just because you haven't updated your look since Adam and Eve were in fig leaves doesn't mean I can't have a little fun with fashion." She opened Hildegard's closet door and pulled out two outfits. "What do you think? The Coco Chanel evening dress? Or maybe the Dior gown, the one they call *Cygne Noir*, the Black Swan? I've been dying to wear it! But maybe I should go with something more professional, as befits my position here at Relationship. Coco has this cute little suit made of worsted wool crepe and lined with silk. It feels totally decadent, and besides, it looks great on me!"

Hildegard stared at the dresses. "How did you do that? An hour ago only my raincoat and galoshes were in that closet." She looked down at her brown tweed suit. "And what's wrong with my look?"

"I'm sure there's nothing wrong with your look...that a bevy of designers working around the clock couldn't fix." Angelica smiled. "I'm going to wear the Black Swan. It's just right for a celebration."

"Don't pop any champagne corks just yet. Things are going well, but you never know."

"Oh come on, Hildy, don't be such a sourpuss. Not only did we get Iris and Riley together, we managed to make our little trip to Earth without getting caught."

"Shhh." Hildy glanced over her shoulder. "We were just lucky. Don't ever mention you-know-what again."

Angelica thought her friend was being paranoid but she was in too good a mood to argue. "All right, if you say so. Still, you have to admit that Iris and Riley have fallen in love. They're going to be together forever."

"I really hope so," Hildegard said. "But I've seen cases before where two mortals seemed perfect for each other and still broke up, even after swearing undying love."

"Well, I think they're in it for the long haul." Angelica didn't want to think of Riley and Iris splitting apart. She'd grown to care deeply for her first match and she couldn't bear the thought of them separating.

"You're right, Angelica," Hildegard said with a smile. "I'm being a nervous Nellie. I'm sure they'll be just fine."

Angelica nodded in agreement, but now that Hildy had brought up the possibility of trouble in paradise, it was all she could think of.

Relationship Division was a far harder assignment than she'd ever anticipated.

Chapter Eight

Riley woke just as the first rays of dawn began to trickle through the curtains in Iris's room. He lay next to her, content to watch her sleep.

He'd never known anyone like her, had never felt this way about anyone else. He loved her with a ferocity that was almost painful. He couldn't imagine his life without her in it.

The urge to wake her up and make love to her again was strong, but Riley resisted. He'd let her sleep. He knew how tired she must be. Riley smiled to himself when he thought of how they'd woken twice during the night to make love. Until Iris, he wouldn't have thought himself capable of such a feat.

Iris made him believe all kinds of things were possible. Like forevers, and happily-ever-afters.

The phone rang, jarring him from his happy thoughts. Riley jumped out of bed and grabbed the cordless phone from the floor along with his pants, hitting the talk button to stop the ringing. Iris moaned, rolled over, and went back to sleep. He slipped into the hallway and quietly shut the door.

Crossing the hall to his room, Riley closed the door and answered the phone. "Hello?" He balanced the phone against his ear as he slipped on his pants.

"Hello?" The caller sounded uncertain. "May I speak to Iris Jennings, please?"

"She's still asleep. Can I take message for her.?"

"Yes. This is Abby Keyser from Columbus Cruise Lines. Could you tell Ms. Jennings that I'll be e-mailing her work address with an itinerary for the new dates we talked about yesterday? Her flight's been confirmed to arrive in Athens at ten p.m. on Saturday. Someone from the cruise lines will meet her at the airport."

Riley's head whirled. It couldn't be true. She couldn't be leaving him in three days

"You mean this Saturday? You must be mistaken. Iris isn't leaving on Saturday."

"Oh, yes. Like I said, we spoke yesterday and she seemed very excited about the new dates. She faxed me her updated contract right away."

Riley squeezed his eyes shut. *Iris is leaving me.* Even though she said she loved him. Even though she'd made love with him.

"You'll be sure to give her my message?"

"Yes. I'll give her the message."

He hit the off button. Intense pain struck him, buckling his knees. He fought against it. For one moment he'd been completely happy. He should have known it wouldn't last.

Had she been planning her escape while she made love to him? Was he no more than a little diversion for her before she left?

Riley held onto his sense of injustice like a protective shield. Maybe if he concentrated on how he'd been used, he wouldn't care that Iris was leaving him in three days.

Maybe it would hurt less if he was the one who did the leaving.

****

Iris woke and gave a languorous stretch. She closed her eyes and images of making love with Riley played in her head, arousing her once more. Iris laughed to herself. She'd never imagined she could turn into such a sex fiend, but being in love with an Adonis of a man seemed to have that affect on her.

With that thought in mind she jumped out of bed. Perhaps she could persuade Riley to come back to bed. She grabbed his uniform shirt from the floor and slipped it on. Iris breathed in Riley's scent and went in search of him.

She found him sitting at the dining room table wearing his uniform, a cup of coffee in front of him. Iris came up behind him and hugged him around his neck. She kissed his cheek.

"Hey, I'm the only one who gets to wear your uniform today. Why don't you come back to bed so I can take it off?"

"When were you going to tell me, Iris?"

The tone of his voice surprised her even more than his question. The barely restrained anger she heard frightened her. She released him and stepped away.

"When was I going to tell you what?"

"Don't play games with me, Iris. When were you going to tell me you were leaving in three days? Your friend, Ms. Keyser from Columbus Cruise Lines, is sending your new itinerary by e-mail. She said you couldn't wait to go."

"The cruise line?" Iris had completely forgotten about promising to leave early. "I'm not going."

"Ms. Keyser says you are."

"Well, screw Ms. Keyser. I'm not going." She touched his arm. "I want to stay with you."

He rose to his feet, shrugging off her touch. "For how long, Iris? A few weeks? A few months? Until something better comes along?"

"No! Why are you saying that? I want to stay with you. I love you."

A muscle worked in his cheek and he swallowed. "I think it's best if I stay at the fire hall until you go."

"Riley, no, you don't understand." She grabbed his arm. "I only said I'd go on the cruise early because I thought there was no hope for us. But now everything is different."

"Why, because we've had sex? It doesn't change anything."

"We made love and it changed everything for me."

Riley's lips compressed into a thin, angry line. He looked somewhere past her shoulder when he spoke. "It doesn't change the fact that if you stayed, someday soon you'd regret it and you'd blame me."

"I'm not going to regret it." Desperation made her put her hands on either side of his face, forcing him to look at her. She couldn't lose him.

"I love you, Riley. I've never told that to another man before. I've never been in love before. All my life I've been looking for a home, and I didn't even know it. You're my home, Riley."

A flash of regret flickered in his eyes, and for one second she thought she'd gotten through to him. But then he placed his big hands around her wrists and gently pulled her hands from his face. He averted his gaze as if he couldn't stand to look at her.

"I'm going to work. I've packed a few things, enough to last until Saturday, until you...you leave. Whiskers can stay like we agreed. I'll look after her."

He was serious. Panic bubbling in her chest, she made a desperate grab for his arm when he turned to go.

"Riley, no! Please believe me, I love you and I want to stay. What do I have to do to convince you?"

"Nothing." Riley gently removed her hand from his arm. "There's nothing you can do to convince me."

He picked up his overnight bag and headed to the door. The reality of the situation slammed into Iris. He was leaving and there was nothing she could do or say to stop him.

It was over before it had a chance to begin.

"Wait," she said, closing her eyes. "This is your house. I'll leave."

"You don't have to do that, Iris. Where will you go?"

"I need to leave," she whispered, barely hanging on to her tears. She couldn't stay, surrounded by his things, knowing he didn't want her. "I'll call my friend Shannon. I'll be gone by the time you get home tonight."

Riley stared at her for a few long moments before finally nodding and looking away.

"If that's what you want. Don't worry about Whiskers. Goodbye, Iris."

With that he walked out of the house.

And out of her life.

For a long time Iris stood totally still, too stunned to move or speak or even breathe. Eventually Buddy nuzzled her hand, bringing her back to the present. He and Whiskers needed to be fed and Buddy needed to go outside.

Buddy followed at her feet as she shuffled through the kitchen. He bolted outside as soon as she opened the back door.

Iris scooped food for both Whiskers and Buddy into their bowls and then went back to the door to let the dog in. She watched them eat for a while and then closed her eyes. She couldn't put off the inevitable any longer. She had to leave.

She picked up the phone from the dining room table where Riley had left it and slowly made her way up the stairs. She sat on the edge of her bed, trying to sort her jumbled thoughts. She called her friend Shannon to see if she could bunk with her for a few days. She was relieved when Shannon said she'd love to have her since Whiskers wasn't accompanying her. It broke her heart to leave her pet behind, but she didn't have much choice. She knew Riley would take good care of her.

"Oh, Riley."

Iris wrapped her arms around her waist and rocked herself on the bed. Why had he pushed her away? Why couldn't he love her?

She cried until she felt raw inside, and had no

tears left. Then slowly she began packing her things, preparing for the next part of her life.

Her life without Riley.

****

Angelica mopped at her tears with a huge hankie, heedless of her running mascara. "Oh, Hildy. You were right. I can't believe he broke up with her. He didn't even give their love a chance." She blew her nose with a loud honk.

Hildegard patted her back. "I had a bad feeling about this. Riley loves Iris, but he's afraid of being abandoned again. Some of those childhood traumas never go away."

Angelica sniffled. "I guess that's true. Poor Riley."

Hildegard sighed. "Poor Iris."

"That's it then," Angelica said with a sigh. "I'll pack my things and report to Service Division right away."

"I'm sorry, Angelica. For what it's worth, I think you would have made a fine employee here in Relationship. You certainly have a knack for making matches."

The waterworks started again. "That means a lot to me, Hildy. I'm sorry I won't be working with you. But I'm even sorrier about Iris and Riley. I wish there was something we could do for them."

A loud knock sounded at Hildegard's office door. When she answered the knock, a large angel stepped through the threshold, folding his enormous wings to keep them from being bent. The smaller wings on his heels folded as well.

He passed a business card to Hildegard. As Angelica leaned over her shoulder to read the card, the words popped off the paper and displayed themselves in thin air, creating a 3-D effect.

"Giorgio Angel," Angelica read aloud. "Messenger Division, First Class. When your message absolutely positively has to get there in a nanosecond." The 3-D effect disappeared, the words resuming their place on the business card. Angelica nodded, impressed.

"Nice card, Giorgio."

Hildegard straightened her jacket. "Yes, very effective. Now, what can we do for you?"

"Ah, but it's what I can do you for, madame." He lifted Hildegard's hand and kissed it. "I have a message for you of the utmost urgency."

Hildegard retracted her hand, her face turning a becoming pink. "What's the message? Who's it from?"

"It's from the Divine Leader himself."

Hildegard's hand fluttered to her throat, her face abruptly paling. Angelica reached for her friend's hand, not feeling so well herself at the moment.

"What's the message?" Hildegard whispered. She squeezed Angelica's hand.

Giorgio opened a long scroll and read. "To Hildegard, Angel Third Class, Relationship Division, and Angelica, angel-in-training. From the Divine Leader." Giorgio cleared his throat before continuing. "Dear Angels. Don't think I didn't see what you did. What's your next move? I'll be watching very closely."

Giorgio cleared his throat once more. "It's not every day I deliver a message from the Divine Leader himself. Do you know what it means?"

"Yes, I'm afraid I do," Hildegard said. "Thank you for bringing us the message, Giorgio." She dropped the expected tip into his outstretched hand. With a small bow, Giorgio folded his wings once more and left her office.

Angelica let out the breath she'd been holding. "What does this mean?"

"It means the Divine Leader knows we made an unauthorized trip to Earth to talk to Iris and Riley and he's got his eye on us. There's nothing more we can do."

"Yes, but he didn't say, 'Don't ever go back to Earth.'"

Hildegard nodded. "That's true."

"He hasn't said he'll punish us. He's not forbidding us to go again, just telling us that he's watching closely."

"Perhaps, but the rules say no contact with the mortals we're trying to match. They are very clear on the subject. What are you thinking, Angelica?"

Angelica took a deep breath. "I'm thinking I'm going back to Earth one last time to convince Iris and Riley they belong together."

"No, you can't! The Divine Leader is watching. You could be permanently banned from Heaven."

Angelica inhaled again and let it out slowly. She wanted to stay in Heaven forever, even if she had to work in Service Division. But she couldn't let Riley and Iris languish in unhappiness for the rest of their lives. She had to help them, regardless of what it might cost her.

"I'm going in, Hildy. Thanks for everything." She started to leave.

"No!" Hildegard grasped Angelica's hand. "I won't let you go alone. I'm going too."

"Hildy, no. You've got too much to lose. I'm just an angel-in-training. Who's going to miss me?"

"I will." Hildegard straightened her jacket and adjusted her glasses. "Now don't argue with me, angel-in-training. I'm your supervisor, remember?"

"Yes, you are." She grasped Hildegard's hands. "But you're my friend first."

Hildegard sniffed a couple of times before composing herself and returning to her no-nonsense manner. "Time is of the essence and we've got a lot of work to do."

"What are we waiting for? Let's go, Hildy."

"Just one thing."

"What's that?"

"Don't call me Hildy."

"Whatever you say." *Hildy.*

"I heard that."

Chapter Nine

Angelica flashed her brightest smile at Iris. "Paris would be wonderful this time of year."

Iris simply stared at her across her desk, her expression flat.

"Yes, it's lovely in springtime," she said without enthusiasm. "Would you like me to book a trip for you now?"

Iris's attitude worried Angelica. She sensed a cauldron of emotions brewing inside the young woman, from sadness and despair to disappointment and anger. Worst of all, Angelica felt she had already given up on Riley.

Angelica gritted her teeth, determined not to fail. She'd get Riley and Iris together if it was the last thing she did.

She ignored Iris's question. "Have you been to Paris?"

"Yes, once." A brief smile flitted across her face. "It's my favorite city in the world."

Ah, that was better. A little enthusiasm. Perhaps there was still hope. Angelica stared into Iris's blue eyes, attempting to bend her to her will as she'd done on her previous visit. The mortal will didn't stand a chance against the power of an angel, even one still with training wheels. Angelica smiled in delight. This angel stuff was awesome.

"Why don't you take Riley there? He'd love to see Paris with you."

Iris blinked, and to Angelica's surprise the connection between them wavered, like a candle flickering in the wind.

Angelica panicked. *This wasn't supposed to happen. Aren't angels supposed to be all-powerful?*

She scrambled to establish her control over Iris, staring deeply into her eyes, and concentrating hard to build trust with her.

"How do you know about Riley?" Iris asked. "And for that matter, how do you know so much about me?"

So much for all-powerful angels. What was going on? What happened to her angel mojo?

"You...you must have mentioned him last time I was here." Angelica blew out an exhausted breath. Iris was making her work much harder this time.

"Did I?" Iris's eyes clouded in confusion.

The connection with Iris grew stronger once more. *Whew, that was better.*

"Yes, I'm sure you did. Why don't you ask Riley to go with you to Paris?"

"Riley doesn't want to go anywhere with me." Iris's chin quivered. "He doesn't want to see me anymore."

"I'm sure that's not true. Go to him. Tell him how much you love him. Tell him you belong together. Fight for him."

Iris shook her head and the tenuous link between them wavered again.

"No, I've already told him how I feel. He won't listen to me, and he won't believe me."

Angelica's link to Iris hung by a thread. In desperation, she reached for Iris's hand, sending soothing warmth from her fingertips to her toes. Iris blinked in surprise at the sensation.

"Listen to me, Iris. He loves you, but he's afraid. Every time he's loved someone, he's lost them. He's afraid he'll lose you too. You have to go to him and convince him that you're not going anywhere."

For a moment, as Iris stared unblinking into her eyes, Angelica thought she'd reached her. Then she pulled her hand from Angelica's, completely severing the connection between them. The link snapped like a dry branch.

"No."

"No? What do you mean no?"

"No!" Iris pounded her small fist on the desk. "Doesn't he know I'm afraid, too? I tried to convince him I'm not going anywhere. I practically threw myself at his feet and begged him to let me stay. I love him but if he can't trust me enough to believe me when I say I want to be with him forever, I don't know what more I can do."

Despair quickly replaced Iris's anger, as she wiped tears from her eyes. "If he really wants me to stay, he has to make the next move."

This wasn't going at all according to plan. Iris wasn't listening to her. Angelica sighed. Last time she'd been so receptive.

Okay then. Angelica straightened her shoulders. If the angel powers weren't working, she'd have to rely on good old Angelica powers of persuasion.

"If you really want to be with Riley, why haven't you contacted Ms. Keyser and told her you won't be going on the cruise?"

Iris blinked in surprise. "I...I don't know."

"I'll tell you why. You're giving yourself a way out. If things don't work out with Riley, then at least you've still got the cruise." Angelica threw her hands up in the air, her bracelets jingling wildly. "No wonder he doesn't believe you've got staying power."

For a moment Iris stared at her in stunned surprise. Then she narrowed her eyes and reached for the telephone.

"You want to see staying power? I'll show you staying power."

She punched some numbers into the phone and a moment later began to speak.

"Ms. Keyser, this is Iris Jennings. I'm sorry, but something's come up and I will not be able to work on the cruise. I'm withdrawing my application." She paused and Angelica could hear a frantic voice on the other end of the line. "I'm sorry to bail on you at this late date, but my decision is final. Goodbye, Ms. Keyser."

Iris hung up the phone with a decisive click and immediately got to her feet.

"Where are you going? What are you doing?"

Iris ignored her questions. She walked toward an office at the back of the building, Angelica following in her wake.

Iris knocked on the open door of the office and the woman inside looked up with a smile.

"Can I talk to you for a minute, Sharon?"

"Of course. Come in. Have a seat." Sharon closed the lid of her laptop. "I can't believe it's your last day with us. We're really going to miss you, Iris. Are you all set to catch your plane for Athens this afternoon?"

Iris sat and smoothed the silky material of her bright red skirt across her lap. "Actually, that's what I wanted to talk to you about. I was wondering if you'd filled my position yet."

Angelica sat in the seat next to Iris, her excitement building. "What are you doing, Iris? What's going on?" Iris tossed her an annoyed glare, and then studiously ignored her.

"No, not yet. I've got some interviews slated for next week, so hopefully I can find someone suitable soon." Sharon smiled. "You're a hard person to replace."

Angelica watched Iris swallow nervously. "What if you didn't have to replace me? What if I didn't go? Could I still work here?"

"Really? Are you serious?" Sharon got to her feet and came around her desk. "Of course you can still work here! But I thought you were all gung ho about this cruise job?"

Iris rose as well. "Yeah, so did I. Turns out I'm not so enthusiastic after all."

"Well, I'm sorry your plans didn't work out the way you'd hoped, but I won't pretend I'm not delighted to have you stay." She enveloped Iris in a hug. "Welcome back, sweetie."

"You're staying?" Angelica jumped from her chair and did a little happy dance. Iris rolled her eyes at her.

"Thank you." Iris pulled out of the older woman's embrace. "Would it be okay with you if I took the rest of the afternoon off? I have a lot of things to look after since I'm not leaving after all." She lowered her gaze and sighed. "And I need to go for a walk, clear my head."

"Of course. You can start fresh again first thing Monday morning. Is everything all right, Iris? Is there anything you want to talk with me about?"

"Thank you, Sharon. I really appreciate your concern. And your friendship. But I think I have to handle this on my own."

"Okay, but if you change your mind, my door's always open."

"Thanks, Sharon. For everything."

Angelica followed on Iris's heels as she walked out of her boss's office and back to her cubicle. She retrieved her purse from the bottom drawer of her desk and slung it over her shoulder.

"This is so awesome. You're staying in Portland! Does that mean you're going to fight for Riley? Where are you going now?"

"Out."

"Are you going to Riley?" Angelica crossed her fingers and toes.

"No!" Iris touched her forehead and grimaced, as if a headache had suddenly hit. "Like I said, I have some things to take care of."

"I'll come with you."

"No! Who you are?" She lowered her voice. "And how come no one but me can hear or see you? People are looking at me as if I'm crazy because I'm talking to myself."

"They can't see me because I don't want them to. Eventually you'll forget you saw me, too. I'm an angel and I'm here for you."

Iris stared at her as if she'd just sprouted horns. "You're an angel?"

"Well, an angel-in-training, actually. I'm in Relationship Division."

"An angel-in-training in Relationship Division," Iris repeated. "And I suppose you came from Heaven?"

"Of course. Where else?"

"Where else indeed." Iris broke out in laughter that verged on the hysterical. Several other agents turned to stare at her.

"Okay, it's official. I've just lost my mind."

"No, Iris. You're perfectly sane. What I've told you is true. I'm an angel and my job is to match you with your soul mate."

"My soul mate?" Her laughter abruptly stopped.

"Yes. Riley is your soul mate, your one and only. You need each other."

Iris bit her bottom lip as if holding back a flood of emotion. But then she took a deep breath, gathering herself.

"Okay, I've heard enough. I'm leaving. Don't follow me."

"But—"

She held up her hand, her expression fierce. "I said don't follow me. Go back to Heaven, or whatever loony bin you came from."

Angelica's heart broke as she watched Iris walk out of the travel agency. She sighed. An angel might be able to lead a mortal to love, but she couldn't make her believe in it.

What did she do now? Time was running out.

She took a deep breath and sent up a silent prayer for strength. It didn't matter what happened to her. She had to do whatever she could to help Iris and Riley.

Angelica followed Iris out the door.

****

Hildegard landed with a thump against the glass front doors of Nathan Jarvis's office building. She huffed in annoyance as she straightened her glasses and rubbed her bruised nose. Blasted locater was on the fritz. She'd have to get it recalibrated as soon as she got home.

Assuming she still had a home to go to.

She put the unsettling thought from her mind. Right now Riley's future took precedence. Her fate would have to wait.

Hildegard made her way inside the office. She smiled at the young receptionist at the front desk.

"You don't see me," she said, waving her hand. "Go on with your work."

The receptionist blinked. "I don't see anyone." She turned her attention back to her computer screen. "I'll continue with my work."

"Good girl."

Hildegard slipped past reception and headed further down the hall. The locater said Riley would be at Nathan's office, but so far he was nowhere in sight. For that matter, neither was Nathan.

A terrible thought struck Hildegard. What if the locater had been wrong? After all, her landing point had been off. Perhaps the locater got Riley's whereabouts wrong as well.

As Hildegard reached Nathan's personal office, she waved her hand in front of his secretary, whose desk sat just outside his door.

"Where is Nathan? Is Riley Benson with him?"

The woman stared at her, her eyes glassy from the temporary trance Hildegard induced.

"Nathan just left with Mr. Benson." She pointed to a window that overlooked the office parking lot. "There they are. They're going to Mr. Benson's house."

Hildegard watched in horror as Riley drove off with Nathan Jarvis. "Oh, fiddlesticks!"

She'd missed him! Not only had the locater given her a rough landing, it had miscalculated her interception time. How could this have happened? Her locater had just been in the shop for its 500,000 hour tune-up. When she got back to Heaven she'd have a serious chat with the Service angel.

No, she wouldn't. She could hardly file a complaint against the service angel when she was making an unauthorized trip to Earth. Right now all she could do was to reset the locater and hope it took her to Riley's house without putting her through a window.

Suddenly the locater's alarm went off. Hildegard's heart sank. She'd set the alarm to warn her if her unauthorized excursion had been detected by Heaven security. If she and Angelica didn't return to Heaven immediately they could be shut out forever.

For a moment Hildegard's desire to help Riley and Iris nearly made her ignore the warning. She dialed Riley's new location into the locater, her finger poised over the enter button. Her hand began to shake. Perhaps if only her fate hung in the balance, she would take her chances. But Angelica deserved a chance to prove herself in Heaven. Hildegard wouldn't risk her friend's future.

With a sigh she pressed the cancel button. They had to return to Heaven, even though she hadn't fulfilled their mission. She and Angelica wouldn't be of much use to Riley and Iris, or anyone else, if they were banned from Heaven and lost all their angel powers.

Hildegard called Angelica on the locater. "Angelica, we have to head back. Immediately. Security knows there's been a breach."

"I can't leave yet! I'm not ready—"

"Angel-in-training, I'm ordering you to abort

your mission and return to Heaven. Do you understand?"

"Yes, Hildegard."

She could hear Angelica's disappointment loud and clear through her small locater. Hildegard's heart fell. Did that mean Angelica had failed at her mission as well?

As soon as she was sure Angelica had arrived back safely in Heaven, Hildegard made her own journey. Moments later she was back in her office, or at least in the closet of her office. She landed in a heap amid Angelica's flouncy designer dresses and spiky shoes.

"Stupid locater."

She crawled out of the closet on her hands and knees, pulled herself to a standing position and brushed herself off. When she straightened she saw Angelica sprawled on top of her filing cabinets.

"Are you okay?" She pulled over a chair to help Angelica down.

"I'm fine," Angelica said, carefully swinging her legs over the side of the filing cabinet and easing herself down. "But I think your locater might have a problem or two."

Hildegard saw the disappointment on her friend's face.

"You didn't get a chance to talk to Iris either."

"Oh, I talked to her. Till she told me to shut up and leave her alone. I was trying to follow her when you called. It was as if she were totally immune to my angel powers this time." Angelica sighed. "I really blew it, Hildy."

"So did I." Hildegard told her about her own misadventures.

"But one positive thing happened. Iris decided not to go on the cruise. She's going to stay in Portland."

"That's great news!"

"Not so great. She's angry with Riley and won't

talk to him."

Hildegard's heart fell. They'd failed Riley and Iris. Now they might never know true happiness.

But the knowledge that she'd failed Angelica distressed Hildegard even more. Because of the stupid bargain she'd made with her, her best friend would be forced to work in Service for the rest of the afterlife. Her talents would be wasted there, and worse, she'd be miserable.

Hildegard burst into sudden, wrenching sobs that shook her body and refused to abate. She hadn't cried since her arrival in Heaven eons ago and her tears felt strange, like a muscle she hadn't exercised in a very long time. This was too much. She couldn't bear to think of Riley and Iris apart, and her heart fell to pieces at the thought of Angelica's unhappiness.

Angelica put her arm around her. "Don't cry, Hildy. Everything will be okay."

"How can you say that? We didn't convince them they belong together. And you'll have to go into Service."

"A certain angel supervisor who shall remain nameless once told me I should have faith in our soul mates. We have to believe they love each other enough to try again. If there was ever a time for faith, it's now."

Hildegard wiped her eyes with the sleeve of her tweed jacket. "You're right. All we can do now is watch over them. And pray."

Angelica snapped her fingers and the Earth window opened wide. "Luckily, I am very good at both of those activities." She gripped Hildegard's hand. "Have faith, angel supervisor."

"I'll do my best, angel-in-training."

****

As Iris walked her mood shifted from anger to despair to hope, and back again. Had she really just turned down the job of a lifetime? Was she crazy?

No. Maybe she'd just come to her senses. She loved her life in Portland. She loved her friends, her job, her cat. How could she have thought she could do better by throwing it all away? Whatever happened between her and Riley, Portland was her home.

Riley. What had she done that was so wrong? She'd never made a secret of her plans to join the cruise. Riley had known she was leaving from the day she'd moved into his house.

But everything changed when they made love.

She couldn't imagine leaving him after that. She'd tried to explain that morning that she no longer planned to go on the cruise but Riley wouldn't believe her. Why wouldn't he believe she would stay?

Because he was afraid. Because he'd lost everyone he'd ever loved.

The words popped unannounced into her memory. Iris shook her head. She had a vague recollection of a conversation about Riley, but when she tried to grasp the reminiscence, it evaporated in a cloud of dust. All that remained was a faint jingling of bracelets. *Riley is your soul mate, your one and only. You need each other.*

Another snippet of half-forgotten conversation. The words reverberated in her head, demanding she pay attention. Perhaps Riley's fear of abandonment kept him from believing that what they had together could be real and lasting. Maybe it was up to her to make him believe in it. And believe in her.

The hurt she'd felt at his rejection fell away. She loved him so much and she knew he loved her, too. Somehow she'd make him believe they belonged together.

Iris abruptly stopped walking and looked around, realizing for the first time where she was. She stood directly in front of Riley's house. Without the rest of her being aware of it, her subconscious had brought her back to him.

She shook her head and laughed. No sense arguing with her subconscious. She took a deep breath as she headed to the house to confront Riley.

But Iris knew something was wrong the minute she stepped on Riley's front porch.

Buddy barked frantically inside the house. He scratched at the door in a desperate attempt to get out. Iris caught the scent of smoke and her heart stopped in her chest.

The house was on fire.

Chapter Ten

In case he didn't already know who owned the black Cadillac, the vanity license plates spelled it out in bold blue lettering.

#1 JOE

Riley gripped the arm rest of Nathan Jarvis's car as they pulled to the curb behind the Cadillac. Anger simmered in Riley's gut like a pot ready to boil over. He was spoiling for a fight.

Who better to receive the benefit of his dark mood than Joe Gardiner?

Nathan unbuckled his seat belt and reached into the back seat to retrieve his brief case. "Are you ready for this?"

"Yeah, I'm ready."

"The worst will soon be over and you'll be able to get on with your life."

Riley stared out the windshield. Getting on with his life seemed like a very bleak prospect. Since Iris left his house three days ago, he couldn't sleep and his appetite had deserted him. His captain thought he was sick, and made him take a couple of days off. The time on his hands only made things worse. He'd fried bacon that morning, usually one of his favorites, and then found he couldn't eat it. At least Buddy had enjoyed it.

Without Iris, his world looked empty.

There was nothing he could do about Iris, but maybe he could take care of Joe Gardiner, once and for all.

"Let's go rescue Mrs. Parker."

Riley took the steps to his neighbor's front door

two at a time. Nathan followed a short distance behind.

Mrs. Parker answered his impatient knock with a look of relief. "Riley, I'm so glad you're here! Come in, come in."

"This is Nathan Jarvis, the lawyer I was telling you about."

Beth Parker extended her hand. "Nice to meet you, Mr. Jarvis. I'm so glad you can help Riley."

"So am I."

Riley and Nathan followed Mrs. Parker into her sunny kitchen at the back of the house. Joe Gardiner sat at the table drinking coffee. When he saw Riley, Gardiner abruptly set his cup on the table, the coffee splashing over the side.

"What are you doing here?"

Riley grinned, pleased to see beads of sweat form on Gardiner's brow.

"I came to visit my neighbor and hopefully sample some of her chocolate chip cookies. If she has some, that is." He winked in Mrs. Parker's direction.

She laughed and set a tin of cookies on the table. "I always have cookies for you, Riley. Would you like coffee?"

"I'd love some."

He sat across from Gardiner and helped himself to a cookie. "Let me make some introductions. Joe, this is my lawyer, Nathan Jarvis, one of the best contract lawyers in Portland. Nathan, this is Joe Gardiner."

Nathan dipped his head briefly, but made no move to shake Gardiner's hand. "Mr. Gardiner."

Gardiner's gaze darted from Riley to Nathan and back again. "Perhaps I should come back another time, Beth. I didn't realize when you called to set up this meeting that you were having...guests."

"I can understand why you wouldn't want witnesses to your little business transaction, but actually, this is the perfect time for you to be here."

Gardiner narrowed his eyes. "What are you talking about?"

Riley accepted a cup of coffee from Mrs. Parker. "Did Mr. Gardiner make you an offer on your house?"

She passed a cup to Nathan. "Yes, he did."

"Did he try to pressure you into accepting his offer?" Nathan asked.

Gardiner's hand shook slightly as he lifted his cup. "I wouldn't dream of pressuring Mrs. Parker!"

"You *were* rather insistent." Mrs. Parker resumed her seat at the table. "You said I had to make a decision today. You said it would be difficult to sell the house in this market in its present condition."

"It's a nice house, but like I told you, it will need a lot of updating." Gardiner sneered at Riley. "The unkempt property next door is bringing down your property values."

"Actually, Irvington is one of the most desirable neighborhoods in Portland, isn't it, Joe?" Riley asked. He struggled to keep his anger under control.

"Well, I wouldn't say—"

"How much did Joe offer you, Mrs. Parker?"

"A lot." She named the figure.

Riley gave a low whistle. "That *is* a lot of money, isn't it?"

Mrs. Parker nodded solemnly. "Yes, it certainly is."

"Are you thinking about accepting his offer?"

"Benson, this is none of your business!" Gardiner's face turned an unhealthy shade of red. "My negotiations with Mrs. Parker are private!"

Riley ignored him. He focused on Mrs. Parker. "*Are* you thinking about it?"

"Well, I might have considered the offer if the real estate agent you recommended hadn't already sold my house for fifty thousand dollars more than what Mr. Gardiner is offering, including her commission."

"What?" Gardiner's coloring went from red to scarlet. "You've sold the house?"

"I tried to tell you, but you kept talking over me." She turned to Riley with a smile. "I'm very grateful to you for all your help, and your...er, warnings."

Gardiner jumped to his feet. "How dare you try to make a fool of me! You won't be laughing when I call in your loan, Benson."

"I wouldn't try that if I were you," Nathan said. He snapped open his briefcase and retrieved a document, handing it to Gardiner with a flourish. "Consider yourself served. We're taking you to court to have the contract you made with Riley declared null and void."

"That's ridiculous! What grounds could you possibly have to overturn a perfectly legal contract?"

"On the grounds that the contract was made using extortion."

"Extortion! Don't be absurd! I don't know what Benson has told you but I certainly entered into that agreement in good faith."

"Your asking price was far more than the going rate in the neighborhood at the time."

"If Benson was stupid enough to pay a higher price, that's not my fault. I was just being a shrewd businessman."

"You threatened to demolish the house if he didn't pay your price."

"That's a lie!"

Nathan produced two more papers. "So these demolition permits from the city, granting you permission to take down the house, were what, a joke?"

Riley got to his feet, too restless to sit any longer. "You took great delight in waving those permits in my face. You told me the house would be demolished if I didn't pay what you wanted and I knew you were bastard enough to do it."

"I'll hire the best lawyers. I'll fight you in court." Sweat ran down Gardiner's left temple as he sank back into his chair.

"That's your prerogative, of course," Riley said, "but I think you'll probably be very busy putting out other fires."

Gardiner pulled a hanky from his pocket and mopped his brow. "What are you talking about?"

"The IRS is investigating you for tax fraud," Nathan said. "They're seizing documents and computers at your office as we speak."

"What?"

"Your insurance company is launching its own investigation. We made them aware of your cash settlement with Iris Jennings. Since they compensated you fully for the damages to the apartment, they weren't pleased to learn you'd been paid twice. It made them wonder what other nefarious insurance claims you might have made." Nathan plucked another document from his briefcase. "We're also suing for the return of Ms. Jennings' money since the settlement was made using coercion."

Gardiner hauled himself awkwardly to his feet and took an unsteady step backward. "I'll fight you; I'll fight you all. I've worked too hard to let anyone take what belongs to me."

Riley stood over Gardiner and looked down into his frightened, sweating face. He enjoyed the discomfort his greater height gave the older man.

"But you haven't heard the best part. Nathan is asking the courts to overturn the original sale between you and my great aunt and uncle. We've got two doctors willing to testify that Claude was in the early stages of Alzheimer's when he signed that contract." Riley's heart pumped wildly and his hands fisted at his sides. "You took advantage of an old, sick man. You're nothing but scum."

"As the Bensons' sole heir, Riley is entitled to inherit the property without owing you a cent," Nathan added.

Gardiner's mouth opened and closed, but no sound emerged.

"It's been a real pleasure talking to you, Joe," Riley said through clenched teeth, "but I think it's time for you to go now. Don't you?"

Riley itched to land a hard right hook into the bastard's face, to feel bones break under his fist. With an effort he forced his hands to unclench. He knew Gardiner would use any violence on his part to undermine the lawsuit. He wouldn't give him the satisfaction.

Gardiner carefully backed away, as if he sensed the fury and anguish seething inside Riley.

"Yes I...I should be going."

Mrs. Parker took him by the arm. "Why don't I show you out?"

As soon as Mrs. Parker and Gardiner left the room, the adrenalin he'd been operating on the last couple of days suddenly deserted Riley, leaving him exhausted. He dropped into a chair, holding his head in his hands.

"Are you all right?" Nathan asked.

He managed a smile. "I'm fine. I'm just glad Gardiner isn't going to be any more trouble for Mrs. Parker."

"Or for you, I hope," Beth said as she reentered the kitchen. "After what he did to you, and to your aunt and uncle, I hope he rots in jail."

Riley chuckled, amused by the vehemence in her voice. "I didn't know you were so bloodthirsty."

Beth shook her head. "I have my moments. But seriously, if you hadn't warned me about him, I could have been his next victim."

"I'm glad I could help."

"I'm going back to the office. I'm expecting a

fight from Gardiner and I want to be ready," Nathan said.

Riley pushed himself to his feet. He extended his hand to Nathan. "Thank you for everything. I can't begin to tell you what it means to me to have this weight off my shoulders."

Nathan clapped him on the back as they walked to the front door. "You're entirely welcome. It was a pleasure to put Joe Gardiner out of commission. I'm going to enjoy dueling with him in court."

"Well, I'm glad you're happy about it since you didn't make a dime for all your trouble."

"Like I told you, Iris is a friend and she thought you were worth it. Where is Iris anyway?"

Just hearing Iris's name caused a painful stab to his heart. He'd have to get used to it. "She's leaving today for her cruise job. Her flight must have left by now. She's not coming back."

"I'm sorry to hear that," Nathan said. He eyed Riley closely. "But unless I miss my guess, I'm not half as sorry as you are."

Riley turned away. "It didn't work out. It's...complicated."

"Too bad. Iris is a great girl. Jill and I will miss her."

Yeah. Me too.

Mrs. Parker opened the front door. "Thank you both for everything. And Riley, why don't you come on over for supper this week? I'll be moving soon and we won't have many more chances to get together."

"I'd like that." Beth must have thought he looked lonely.

How pathetic was that?

He was happy Beth Parker's financial future looked secure, and more than pleased Gardiner would soon get what he deserved.

But despite the fact that for the first time in two years his financial situation was turning a corner, the pleasure he might have experienced felt muted, as if he was no longer capable of feeling joy.

Iris is leaving today and I'll never see her again.

He said his goodbyes to Nathan and Beth, and stood for a moment on Beth's front porch after she'd gone back inside her house and Nathan had driven away. Now what? The thought of going home to his empty house made him shiver, despite the warm afternoon.

But his house wasn't entirely empty. Buddy and Whiskers needed to be fed and cared for. Life went on. He walked around the side of Beth's house to the back alley.

The wind suddenly changed direction, bringing a new, and familiar, smell.

Smoke. Something close by was on fire.

Riley ran back to Beth's house, and took the stairs up to the raised deck off the back door of her house. From this high point he hoped to see the tell-tale signs of smoke. If he could see smoke, maybe he could find the fire and call 911. The sound of a barking dog made him turn his attention toward his own house next door.

Riley's heart stopped.

Smoke billowed from his open back door. Buddy barked frantically and ran in circles around someone attempting to drag a garden hose through the open door.

Not someone. *Iris.*

Iris was walking into his house. His burning house.

Riley banged his fist against Beth's back door. When she opened it, he turned and raced back down the stairs, yelling over his shoulder.

"Call 911. My house is on fire."

He sprinted across the lawn, his only thought to save the woman he loved.

****

"Oh my gosh, Hildy!" Angelica grabbed Hildegard's arm. "What have we done? We've made things worse! We've put both Iris and Riley in danger!"

"Don't panic, Angelica. Riley's smart, and he's a firefighter. He'll know what to do."

"I hope you're right, Hildy." But Angelica's well of optimism was running a little low.

A loud knock sounded at Hildegard's office door and both angels started in surprise.

"Are you expecting anyone?" Angelica asked.

"No." Hildegard stepped to the door, her face full of trepidation. "Who is it?

"Giorgio, Messenger Angel, First Class."

"Quick! Close the Earth window," Hildegard whispered. Angelica closed the window with a snap of her fingers and Hildegard opened her office door.

"Welcome, Giorgio. Come in."

Giorgio folded his enormous wings and stepped inside. He held out his business card, but Hildegard shook her head. "We've seen the card, Giorgio. What brings you back here?"

"I am bringing you a message, of course. From the Divine Leader himself. That's twice in one day."

Hildegard gave him a tight smile. "From the Divine Leader? How...lovely."

Giorgio eyed them suspiciously. "I don't know what you did to warrant another message from the Divine Leader, but I'd be worried if I were you."

"Save the condescension and just read the message, Giorgio," Angelica said in annoyance.

"Of course." Giorgio gave her a mocking bow and unfurled his scroll.

"To Hildegard, Angel Third Class, Relationship Division and Angelica, angel-in-training, from the Divine Leader. This is what happens when you interfere. Things don't always go the way you expect, especially when you are dealing with mortals. What lessons have you learned? Giorgio will wait for your reply."

Angelica and Hildegard stared at each other.

Giorgio stood poised with his feather quill and scroll. He lifted an eyebrow when neither of them spoke.

"Well? The Divine Leader is waiting."

"Yes, of course." Hildegard's brow knitted together as she thought. "I've learned that I'm not always right. Other people's ideas are often better than mine."

"I've learned that angels can't make mortals fall in love, or stay together, no matter how right we believe they are for each other," Angelica added.

Hildegard nodded. "I guess that's why we have the 'No Contact' rule in the policy manual. We can introduce them to potential soul mates but only they can decide who they want to love."

"I've learned that friendship is the most important thing of all," Angelica said, taking Hildegard's hand.

"Yes, friendship is important." Hildegard smiled. "And friends are to be treasured."

"And friends are to be treasured," Giorgio repeated as he wrote. He lifted his quill. "Is that everything?"

Angelica looked at Hildegard and nodded. "Yes, I think that pretty much says it all."

Giorgio's scroll rolled itself into a neat bundle. "I shall deliver your reply immediately. Please wait here for your answer." He folded his wings once more and left.

"Quick!" Hildegard said, as soon as he closed her office door. "Open the Earth window! What have we missed?"

Angelica flung open the window. The window was gray with smoke and nothing else was visible. Hildegard coughed as the smoke drifted through the open window and began to fill the office.

"Rewind, rewind! Let's find out what's going on!"

Angelica's hands trembled as she pressed the rewind button. She closed her eyes and sent a prayer to the Divine Leader. *Please, please let Riley and Iris be okay.*

****

Iris fumbled in her purse until she found the house key she hadn't returned. The moment she opened the door, Buddy and Whiskers dashed into the front yard, followed by a billow of smoke. Iris tried to see inside the house but the thick smoke pushed her back. *Dear God. Please make Riley be at work. If he's in the house...*

Iris fought back panic and tried to think clearly.

She wanted to call the fire department, but she didn't have a phone. If she ran around the neighborhood looking for a phone, the house may be lost while she wasted time. She had no choice but to act on her own.

Her decision made, she ran to the back door. Buddy followed her, barking madly. She grabbed the garden hose and turned on the water, hoping it was enough to save Betty. Riley would be devastated if he lost her.

Had Riley told her he had a shift at the fire hall on Saturday? Iris couldn't think clearly enough to remember. Oh God, how could he survive with all that smoke?

No. Iris had to believe he was safe or she couldn't go on.

She opened the back door and aimed the garden hose at the kitchen. No flames were visible through the thick smoke and Iris hoped that meant the destruction was limited to smoke damage. If she went further inside maybe she could put out the fire before it did much more harm. She couldn't let Riley's precious home burn. She had to save it. Filling her lungs with clean air she stepped inside.

****

Knock-knock!

Both angels recognized Giorgio's impatient rap.

"Oh no, just when we were going to find out what happened to Iris!" Angelica groaned.

"I have to let him in," Hildegard said. "Close the window. We'll check in again as soon as he leaves."

"Yes, you're right. Good luck, Hildy."

"Good luck, Angelica."

Hildegard opened the door and once more Giorgio stepped inside, filling the small space with his presence.

"Hildegard, Angel Third Class and Angelica, angel-in-training, I have news." Giorgio lifted his nose and sniffed the air. "What is that unpleasant smell?"

Angelica waved her hand behind her back to dissipate the smoke. "Smell? What smell? Do you smell anything Hildy?"

"Ah no, just your perfume, Angelica."

Giorgio looked at Angelica with distaste. "You should try a new scent. This one is very disagreeable."

"I'll take that under advisement."

"What do you have for us, Giorgio?" Hildegard asked.

Giorgio unfurled the first of two scrolls he held in his hands. "I have two messages for you."

"Two messages?"

"The first message is from Avenger Division." Giorgio cleared his throat. "To Hildegard, Relationship Division. As per your memo regarding the mortal Joe Gardiner, we have carefully examined this case and have concluded that your concerns are well founded. Mr. Gardiner will pay for his crimes on Earth, and you can be certain he will continue to pay in the afterlife. Signed, Avenger Division, Retribution Department."

"Oh, that is good news, Hildy," Angelica said. "Gardiner's going to get what he deserves."

"It's all about justice, on Earth and in the afterlife." Hildy took a deep breath and turned to Giorgio. "You said you had two messages."

"Indeed I do. The second is your answer from the

Divine Leader."

Angelica reached for Hildegard's hand, squeezing her fingers for reassurance. Hildegard nodded at the messenger, her voice trembling slightly.

"Please relay the message, Giorgio."

"To Hildegard, Angel Third Class, Relationship Division and Angelica, angel-in-training. From the Divine Leader." Giorgio paused and looked at them. "Are you sure you're ready?"

"Yes!" they shouted in unison.

"Okay, okay." He found his place again. "From this day forward Hildegard shall be known as Angel Second Class. Congratulations on your promotion."

For a moment Angelica and Hildegard were too stunned to speak. Angelica recovered first.

"Hildy, you got a promotion! Congratulations!"

"Are you sure you read that right, Giorgio?"

"It was delivered perfectly," he said haughtily, "but I'm not done. There's more."

"Please continue."

"To Angelica, angel-in-training," he read. "I feel she will be an asset in Relationship Division and shall start work immediately. In addition, I have decided she be enrolled part-time in Heaven University in order to gain higher training in the angel arts."

"Angelica, this is fantastic! Congratulations! I couldn't be happier for you." Hildegard embraced Angelica in a warm hug.

"Excuse me." Giorgio lifted his chin with an air of snooty self-importance. "It is quite rude to interrupt, you know."

Hildegard gave Angelica a surreptitious wink. "Oh. I'm terribly sorry, Giorgio. Please continue."

He noisily cleared his throat. "Angelica and Hildegard have received these promotions because they have learned an essential lesson: Angels cannot make mortals fall in love. Mortals must figure out for themselves who they love and angels can't change that, no matter how much they may want to.

"Both angels have shown a willingness to sacrifice their own happiness and well-being to help others and each other. However, Angelica still exhibits a mortal-like tendency toward vanity. In the future I shall be closely monitoring her. Signed, the Divine Leader." With a snap of his fingers, Giorgio's scroll spun itself into a neat bundle once more. "Well, you really pulled that one out of the fire. Angel-in-training, consider new perfume. You are quite obnoxious. Good day, ladies."

Hildegard gave him his tip and he was gone. She turned to Angelica.

"Do you know what this means?" she asked.

"That I get to stay in Heaven," Angelica said in relief. "Did he really say I can work here in Relationship Division with you?"

"Yes, he really did. And you'll go to Heaven U part-time. Isn't that exciting?"

Angelica puffed out her chest. "I'll be the best student they've ever had."

"You might want to tone down the vanity switch a notch or two. Remember, the Divine Leader is watching you."

"Oh yes, you're right." She looked upward. "Sorry about that. I'm working on it." She turned to Hildegard. "Do you think I can start decorating my office now that I'm official?"

Hildegard grinned. "Oh, why not? You deserve it. There's a small office down the hall you can have. You can paint it as purple as you like."

Angelica clapped her hands in glee. "Thank you, Hildy. You're a good friend."

"I've been meaning to talk to you about something," Hildegard said.

"What's that?"

"About how you call me Hildy."

"Oh yes, I keep forgetting that you don't like

being called that. I'm sorry. I promise I won't do it again."

"It's okay," Hildegard said. "It's starting to grow on me. Maybe I can teach you proper angel etiquette and you can teach me to loosen up a bit. You can even give me fashion advice. What do you think?"

Angelica smiled. "You help me and I help you. I think that's what friends are for."

"Good." Hildegard clasped Angelica's hand, her smile disappearing. "Omigosh, in all the excitement we forgot about Riley and Iris! Quick, open the Earth window again!"

"Don't worry," Angelica said as she flung open the window once more. "I have a very good feeling that they're going to get their own happily ever after."

****

Iris took one more step inside the house, holding the sleeve of her jacket over her mouth and nose to prevent inhaling the thick, acrid smoke. Her eyes stung. She couldn't hold her breath much longer. But she had to save Betty for Riley.

"Iris!"

Her heart stopped. She turned around and saw Riley in the doorway. He grabbed her arm and pulled her out. Buddy barked furiously at their feet.

Riley led her into the back yard, his fingers squeezing hers painfully. When they were a short distance away from the house, he grasped her shoulders and shook her.

"What the hell were you doing? You never, never, go into a burning building."

"Riley, the house! We've got to save it!"

"Never mind the damn house." He expelled a breath and closed his eyes. "Iris, if something had happened to you..."

"I was afraid you were in the house." Tears poured down her face but she was helpless to stop them. She touched his face. "Thank God you're all right."

He swore and dragged her into his arms. Iris clung to him. She was vaguely aware of the sound of sirens approaching, but nothing else mattered. Riley was safe in her arms.

"You didn't go," he said.

"No."

He put a little space between them and lifted her chin so he could look into her eyes. "Why didn't you go on the cruise? You've been looking forward to it for weeks."

"Because you're here. You're my home, Riley, my life."

He looked confused. "So you're staying? You're not leaving later to catch up with the cruise?"

"No. I told Ms. Keyser I was no longer interested in the cruise. I'm staying in Portland. It's where I belong." Iris laughed through her tears. "Short of being hit by a bus, I plan to be around for a long time. With you."

"You really mean that, don't you?" His face held an expression of total astonishment.

"With all my heart."

Riley looked toward the house. Iris followed his gaze. Firefighters were dragging hoses inside the house.

"Oh my God!" he said suddenly. "I think I forgot to turn off the hotplate after I fried bacon this morning." He stared at the smoke billowing from the back door, shaking his head in disbelief. "I started the fire."

Iris couldn't help it. She laughed. "I know exactly how you feel. Don't worry, sweetheart. If any of the other firefighters ask, you can tell them I started it. I'm sure they'll believe it."

He looked at Iris and smiled. "It doesn't matter. Nothing matters except that you're safe and with me."

"It matters to me and I know how much the

house means to you," Iris said gently, touching his face. She loved the feel of his stubble under her fingers. "The last few weeks I've grown very close to Betty."

He kissed her upturned face, and wiped away the last of her tears. "Yeah, you're right. I've got a lot of memories tied up in that old house. But if it was a choice between you or Betty, I'd let her burn to the ground. No question."

His eyes were fierce with conviction and Iris knew he meant it. Her heart filled with happiness and love.

"I'm glad it didn't come down to that choice. We're both going to be okay."

"Thank God." He pulled her close. "By the looks of it, she'll need a good cleaning and some repairs from the damage I've caused her. I'm glad I've got fire insurance."

"Maybe we can take a little trip while Betty gets back in shape. Paris is beautiful this time of year. I'd love to show it to you."

"What if we make it a honeymoon in Paris? Will you marry me, Iris?"

Iris blinked back fresh tears, her heart overflowing with joy. "I thought you'd never ask."

Riley kissed her, and then sighed as he watched the firefighters hosing down the house.

"Even if the insurance covers the cleanup, there's still a lot of work left to be done on the house. Are you sure you know what you're in for? Are you sure Portland is where you want to stay?"

Iris kissed him back. "Portland, Paris, Poughkeepsie, it doesn't matter. As long as you're with me, I don't care if we live in a car. You're my home Riley. I love you."

"I love you too, Iris." He laughed as he lifted her off her feet and twirled her around. "Welcome home, sweetheart."

Jana Richards has tried her hand at many writing projects over the years, from magazine articles and short stories to paranormal suspense and romantic comedy. She loves to create characters with a sense of humor, but also a serious side. She believes there's nothing more interesting than peeling back the layers of a character to see what makes them tick.

When not writing up a storm, working at her day job as an Office Administrator, or dealing with ever present mountains of laundry, Jana can be found on the local golf course pursuing her newest hobby.

Jana lives in Western Canada with her husband Warren, along with two university-aged daughters and a highly spoiled pug/terrier cross named Lou.